Orphans Preferred

Renée Vajko Srch

Illustrated by Faythe Payol

Orphans Preferred by Renée Vajko Srch
Copyright © 2021. All rights reserved.

ALL RIGHTS RESERVED: No part of this book may be reproduced, stored, or transmitted, in any form, without the express and prior permission in writing of Pen It! Publications, LLC. This book may not be circulated in any form of binding or cover other than that in which it is currently published.

This book is licensed for your personal enjoyment only. All rights are reserved. Pen It! Publications does not grant you rights to resell or distribute this book without prior written consent of both Pen It! Publications and the copyright owner of this book. This book must not be copied, transferred, sold or distributed in any way.

Disclaimer: Neither Pen It! Publications, or our authors will be responsible for repercussions to anyone who utilizes the subject of this book for illegal, immoral or unethical use.

This is a work of fiction. The views expressed herein do not necessarily reflect that of the publisher.

This book or part thereof may not be reproduced in any form, stored in a retrieval system, or transmitted in any form by any means-electronic, mechanical, photocopy, recording or otherwise-without prior written consent of the publisher, except as provided by United States of America copyright law.

Published by Pen It! Publications, LLC in the U.S.A.
812-371-4128 www.penitpublications.com

ISBN: 978-1-63984-143-1
Edited by Dina Husseini
Cover Design by Donna Cook

Dedication

This one is for you, Laura O'Connor,
My smart and beautiful niece.
In many ways Billy reminds me of you;
Determined, hard-working, and blessed with a kind and loving heart.
Love you!

As always, thank you to illustrator Faythe Payol who does such a fantastic job of bringing my books to life.

Acknowledgements

A special thanks to my publisher, Debi Stanton, for her assistance in getting this book published.

Thank you to all who helped by reading, editing, and offering suggestions, especially Gail O'Connor, Elijah Knipp, Billy Jean Weinert, and Melissa and Philip Festervand.

Thank you to my friend, Eldon Orme, who rode the Pony Express trail and provided materials that were very helpful.

Thank you to my wonderful and supportive husband, Leonard Srch, who proofreads each revision, and thank you to my three sons, Andrew, Benjamin, and Christopher, who have learned to deal with Mom's creative moods!

I love you dearly!

Table of Contents

Chapter One 1
Chapter Two 7
Chapter Three 13
Chapter Four 19
Chapter Five 25
Chapter Six 31
Chapter Seven 37
Chapter Eight 41
Chapter Nine 47
Chapter Ten 53
Chapter Eleven 57
Chapter Twelve 63
Chapter Thirteen 73
Chapter Fourteen 79
Chapter Fifteen 83
Chapter Sixteen 89
Chapter Seventeen 95
Chapter Eighteen 101
Chapter Nineteen 107
Chapter Twenty 115
Chapter Twenty-One 121
Chapter Twenty-Two 127

Chapter Twenty-Three	135
Chapter Twenty-Four	141
Chapter Twenty-Five	147
Chapter Twenty-Six	153
Chapter Twenty-Seven	161
Chapter Twenty-Eight	169
Chapter Twenty-Nine	175
Chapter Thirty	179
Chapter Thirty-One	183
Chapter Thirty-Two	187
Chapter Thirty-Three	191
Chapter Thirty-Four	197
Chapter Thirty-Five	201
Chapter Thirty-Six	207
Chapter Thirty-Seven	211
Chapter Thirty-Eight	217
Epilogue	221
Historical Note	225
Bibliography	227

Chapter One

"You the hired hand goin' to Mud Springs?" a tall, broad-shoulder man called through the darkness.

"Yes, sir," I said, hurrying down the boardwalk. Julesburg, a town usually bustling with people, was dark and eerily quiet this morning. No one was up at such an early hour other than the two of us.

"You're late."

"I'm sorry sir. I wasn't sure what time...."

The man waved a hand. "Never mind. Jus' get in."

Grabbing the wet, metal seat rail, I swung up, dropping onto the hard, wooden bench beside him.

"Name's Hammond," the driver said, reaching under the seat to pull out an oil cloth much like the one he was wearing. "Put this on."

With a jolt that took me by surprise, we took off. Drenched from the quarter mile walk into town, I didn't really see the need for an oilcloth but went ahead and draped it over my head and shoulders anyway.

For a while, we rode in silence, the wind and the rain making it hard to talk. I was relieved, glad not to have to answer any awkward questions just yet.

Leaning back on the seat, I tried to relax, snuggling my carpetbag closer against my chest to keep it dry. It didn't contain much, just a few clothes, my bowie knife, and Ma's Bible. It was the only memento I had of the woman who had brought me into this world, and I didn't want it to get ruined by the rain.

After a bit, the rain clouds moved out and the wind died down to a breeze.

"Best to set these to dry," Mr. Hammond said, taking off his oil cloth then draping it across the wagon bed.

I nodded, spreading my oil cloth next to his. I hadn't slept well so I was having a hard time staying awake. A thunderstorm had rolled in last night, just as I was dozing off. Big fat raindrops beat down hard on the barn roof, as though some giant were knocking, wanting to come in.

Once the storm had moved on, I'd drifted off, my sleep troubled by nightmares. I dreamt I was stuck knee-deep in mud, struggling to free myself, yet sinking deeper and deeper. In my dream, Pa stood over me yelling, "Yer good fer nothin', Billy. Good for nothin'."

I'd awoken, scared and shaken, uncertain what time it was. With Mr. Brigg's rooster off hiding somewhere because of the storm and no clock to check the time, I'd decided to get up and walk the quarter mile into town. Now I was glad I did because it was later than I'd thought, and I'd nearly missed my ride.

The rhythmic clip-clop of the horses' hooves and the creaking of the wagon gradually lulled me to sleep. My head drooped forward.

A-woooo. A-woooo.

My eyes snapped open. "W... what's ... that?"

Reaching under the seat, Mr. Hammond pulled out a double-barreled shotgun. "Wolves."

I shivered. "Have.... Have ya ever needed to use that?"

He pulled back the hammer, setting the rifle across his lap. "Not yet, but I been told the wolves in these parts are bigger'n mules with teeth the size of arrowheads. Out here's no place to be caught without a weapon."

The mares faltered in their stride, muscles taut, ears pricked backwards as a second bloodcurdling howl carried up into the night. A chorus of chilling cries joined in, echoing through the darkness.

"Easy, girls," Mr. Hammond murmured, his voice dropping an octave, his words measured and slow. "We gonna be jus' fine."

Head high, nostrils wide, the mares kept moving, their pace choppy as the wolves continued to call back and forth. The wolves' feral, deep-throated cries swelled to a loud, visceral chorus until a hair-raising scream ripped through the night.

An eerie silence followed, hovering over the land like a dark cloud.

I was shaking so much. My boots beat a rapid staccato against the dash. *Tap, tap, tap.*

"You okay, boy?"

"Y... yea," I stammered, licking my lips. I could taste the bile in my throat.

"Them wolves can be scarry sometimes," Mr. Hammond muttered, tucking his rifle under the seat. "You'll get used to 'em."

I didn't answer but kept my doubts to myself.

The rose tint of dawn finally drove back the dark, menacing night, bringing with it a sense of relief. In every direction, vast expanses of prairie stretched as far as the eye could see. Trees were scarce, leaving the grassland and the creatures who lived here exposed to predators and fierce weather.

"See them tracks?" Mr. Hammond said, pointing to twin ruts in the ground.

I nodded.

"They's been made by all them wagons headin' west. People followin' a dream."

Then he pointed to a mound of rocks marked with a simple cross of twigs tied together with a piece of string.

"There's the grave of some poor soul who didn't make it. It's a rough journey. Too many times it's the little ones who are lost along the way."

I wrapped my arms around my chest as his words struck me. I wasn't much different from these people who had chosen to give up their homesteads, their families, their friends, and most of their belongings, just to chase a dream, hoping for a better life.

The sun climbed higher in the sky, balmy and pleasant. I set my bag under the seat then took off my coat, draping it over the side of the wagon.

"So, what's your name?" Mr. Hammond asked, fishing out a tobacco pouch from his pocket.

I slid off my boots, propping my wet feet on top of the dash to dry. "Billy," I said, turning sideways on the hard bench to see him better.

Mr. Hammond gave me a hard look as he loosened the drawstring. "Now don't ya go tellin' anyone. I signed the Pony Express oath good as the next man; no drinkin', smokin', chewin' tabacca', cursin' or fightin'. But a man's gotta do somethin' to pass the time."

Dipping his thumb and index finger into the pouch, he removed a pinch of tobacco, then wedged it in one cheek.

"So, what made ya sign up to work at Mud Springs?" he asked, switching the wad of tobacco from one cheek to the other.

I thought about the past couple of weeks. How much could I tell this stranger? He seemed like a nice man, yet I had to watch what I said. I couldn't let anyone know who I really was, nor anything about my past. I had too many secrets I needed to keep safe. My life depended on it.

I replied. "I didn't."

Chapter Two

Settling back as best I could on the hard bench, I told him my story. At least the parts I could reveal without putting my life in danger.

"Two days ago, I noticed a sign in the window of Julesburg's General Store," I began.

The sign read:'

> PONY EXPRESS
> St. Joseph, Missouri to California
> In 10 days or less
> **WANTED!**
> YOUNG, SKINNY, WIRY FELLOWS
> NOT OVER EIGHTEEN
> Must be expert riders
> Willing to risk death daily.
> Orphans preferred.
> WAGES $25 PER WEEK
> Contact Mr. Slade

Wow! Twenty-five dollars a week! I'd thought. Heck, I'd carry the mail clear through to California for that kind of money!

Bursting into the General Store, I ran to the counter where Mr. Rivers usually stood, stocking shelves or helping customers. Behind the counter, shelves ran floor to ceiling, packed tight with bolts of material, pots and pans, salt, flour, sugar, hammers, nails, coffee, and most anything a homesteader might need. My favorite shelf, right behind the cash register, was lined with glass jars filled with lemon drops, sorghum drops, pralines, peppermint sticks, glazed pecans, candied peels, and almond stuffed dates drizzled with honey.

This day, however, Mr. Rivers wasn't there. Instead, a boy about my age sat on a stool behind the cash register, head propped on one hand. The other hand held a pencil which he drummed against the counter.

Tap, tap, tap.

"'scuse me," I said. "Is Mr. Rivers here?"

The boy gave me a blank look. "Went home fer lunch."

He sniffled, swiped the back of his hand across his nose, then started drumming again.

Tap, tap, tap.

"How soon ya think he'll be back?"

"Dunno. Maybe an hour, maybe more."

Oh, how I wanted to snatch that annoying pencil out of his hand! I shoved my hands in my pockets instead.

"Can ya help me, then?"

They boy shrugged.

"Saw the sign in yer window 'bout the Pony Express. Do ya know where I can find Mr. Slade?"

"He's stayin' at the boardin' house fer now."

"Where's that?"

"Across from the barber's shop. Heard he's leavin' soon. Ya better hurry."

"Thanks," I called over my shoulder, racing out the door.

The barber shop, with its red and white striped pole, was the last building on the west end of Main Street. Across the road stood a two-story clapboard house with a sign that advertised rooms for twenty-five cents a night.

Dashing across the road, I nearly ran into a young man coming out of the boardinghouse. He was whistling *Old Dan Tucker*, thumbs hooked through his belt loops.

"Whoa there, young fella," he said, stepping to one side. "What's the rush?"

"Is... Do you know if Mr. Slade is in?" I stammered.

"Jus' talked to him."

He was smartly dressed in tan trousers tucked into high-topped boots and a close-fitting jacket. A red bandana was knotted around his neck. A cowboy hat, pulled low over a tangle of ginger curls, shaded his face. In one hand he held a pair of buckskin gloves.

"Room one, right at the top of the stairs."

I nodded. "Thank you."

My pulse quickened as I climbed the narrow stairway. On the landing, I ran a hand through my hair then straightened my collar. I sucked in a deep breath then knocked on the door.

No answer.

I rapped louder.

"Come in!" a gruff voice bellowed.

Swallowing the lump in my throat, I opened the door and peered inside. A tall, slender man paced back and forth in front of the bedroom window. A crumpled paper clutched in his fist. Without turning to look at me, the man continued his pacing, mumbling words I couldn't make out. I cleared my throat loudly.

The man whirled around. He gave me a sharp, piercing look that made my legs go weak.

"You need something, boy?" he snapped.

I tried to speak but couldn't for the lump in my throat.

The man glared at me. "What do you want, boy?"

"I... I'm here about the job."

"Come on in and shut the door."

I did as he asked, then leaned against the door for support. The man didn't utter a word but studied me with the intensity of a cat watching a mouse.

A knot tightened in my stomach. "Are you Mr. Slade?"

"Of course," he said. He had a narrow face with thick eyebrows that arched over dark, deep-set eyes. "And you are...?"

At this point, I paused my story, shifting on the hard wooden bench to give myself time to think. Mr. Hammond threw me a questioning look. "And?"

Truth was, I'd been caught off-guard when Mr. Slade had asked me that question. Up until then, no one had cared two bits who I was. I'd been tempted to give him my real name but that was too risky. Glancing over his shoulder, I'd spotted the red and white barber sign.

"I told him my name, Billy Barber."

"Do you have any family, Mr. Barber?" Mr. Slade had asked.

"No, sir," I'd answered. It was an easy lie.

Beside me, Mr. Hammond continued to press, eager to hear the rest of my story. "So...?"

I cleared my throat. "So, I told him my name is Billy Barber. Then Mr. Hammond asked where I was working. I told him I had a temporary job at the livery until Mr. Brigg's foot healed."

Mr. Slade had turned away, crumpling the paper he'd held into a tight wad, then tossed it across the room. "Well, Mr. Barber, I'm afraid you're too late. I've just filled the last position."

My shoulders had slumped in disappointment. I suspected he was judging me based on my stature. Granted, I was short for my age, but I could do a man's work. What I had to do was convince him of that.

I turned back. "I can do the job, sir. Jus' give me a chance. I'll prove it."

Mr. Slade spun on his heels. "I thought I told you the position has been *filled*."

"Can't ya take my name in case one of the riders quits or gits injured?"

"You are a very persistent boy, aren't you? But I have all the riders I need. Good day, Mr. Barber."

Mr. Slade strode across the room, placed a hand firmly on the small of my back, then steered me out the door.

It closed behind me with a click.

Chapter Three

I fell silent as we approached a small cluster of buildings. A tall man emerged from a double-crib barn. Nearby, a small shack huddled against a hillock. Three of its walls were made of mud, brush and grass. The back wall was the rocky slope against which the shack had been built. Canvas sacks, sewn together like a quilt, hung over the doorway.

I shoved my feet back into my boots. "Is this…?"

Mr. Hammond slowed the horses. "Lodgepole station."

I breathed a sigh of relief. Not that I expected much from Mud Springs station. I hoped the place would offer a little more than these crude living conditions. One strong storm and the shack would be nothing but a pile of rubble.

Once the wagon came to a stop, I hopped down, my backside sore from the hard wooden bench.

"Howdy, Mr. Parker," Mr. Hammond said, shaking hands with the man who had come to meet us. Mr. Hammond turned towards me. "Mr. Parker is the manager here at Lodgepole station."

I offered him a faint smile, trying not to stare at the angry red scar running from his left ear down to his mouth. The left half of his lips were sewn together. A black patch covered his left eye.

Mr. Hammond nodded. "This here's Billy Barber. He's gonna help Mr. Perkins at Mud Springs station."

Mr. Parker gave me a curt nod. "Howdy."

Mr. Hammond began lifting heavy sacks off the wagon. "How's the crik today?"

"Too much rain. Creek's up." The station manager's words slurred together, spoken out of the right side of his mouth. "Use the old Indian ford downstream. Bit shallower there."

While a couple of ranchmen switched out the horses, the three of us unloaded several bags of potatoes, dried beans, a jug of molasses, some slabs of cured meat, a couple tins of coffee, a shovel, a bag of nails, and lye soap.

Minutes later, Mr. Hammond and I clambered back onto the wagon. With a lurch, we resumed our westward journey.

"What happened to Mr. Parker?" I asked, once we were out of earshot.

"Tangled with a bear. Woke up one day staring at the inside of the bear's mouth. Good thing he had his gun next to 'im. Shot the beast without seein' where he was aimin'. Nothing short of dumb luck he shot the bear 'stead of himself. Took more'n fifty stitches to sew his face together."

Although the day was warm, I shivered. Goosebumps rose along my arms and legs. So far, everything I'd seen and heard hinted at a wild, hostile land.

"Why's the station called Mud Springs?" I asked over the groans and squeaks of the wagon.

"According to what I heard; a group of travelers stumbled upon the springs right after a herd of buffalo wandered into the water. Stirred up the bottom with their hooves, turning it to mud."

"How 'bout Mr. Perkins, the manager? What's he like?"

"Reckon I don't know much 'bout 'im. Keeps mostly to 'imself. Hard worker though. His hired hand, Tom, only lasted three weeks. Two of 'em got into an ugly fight. One day, Tom saddled one of the horses and took off, angry as a hornet."

I wondered about Mr. Perkins. What kind of man was he? What would happen if we didn't get along? Would Mr. Perkins expect more than I could handle?

The rumble I'd noticed for the past few minutes had grown louder. "Rush Creek's a bit rowdy today," Mr. Hammond said. "Normally she's a quiet little thing but with all the rain we been havin', she's feisty as a wild colt."

Swollen from recent rains, the creek was a force to be reckoned with. Swift and strong, the water thundered past with unbridled force, sucking twigs, branches, leaves, and mud from its banks into its swirling brown current.

Surely, Mr. Hammond wouldn't attempt to cross it. Yet I hoped he wouldn't turn back. The thought of waiting at Lodgepole station till the creek quieted down wasn't a pleasant thought.

"Whoa, there, girls," Mr. Hammond called out as the mares tossed their heads.

Reining them about, he guided the horses downstream to the ford Mr. Parker had mentioned. The creek seemed shallower here, built up with rocks along the bottom and up the channel sides.

Mr. Hammond handed over the reins. "Hold the horses while I check the current." He waded into the creek up to mid-calf, then trudged back out.

"Current's still a bit lively but these girls can handle it, can't ya?" he said, stroking the mares' heads.

I scrambled down then turned over the reins. The last thing I wanted was to be on the wagon if it tipped over.

Mr. Hammond coaxed the horses down the slippery embankment. The mares threw their heads as Mr. Hammond hauled on the halter. "Awe, c'mon girls. It ain't that bad."

The horses stepped into the creek, took a few steps, then set their feet.

Shoving my hand into my pocket, I fished out the apple I'd saved from last night's supper. I knew horses loved a sweet treat. Maybe I could use the apple to lure them across.

Slicing the fruit in half with my bowie knife, I waded into the creek. The rocks lining the riverbed were coated with silt which made them slick. In a flash, my feet slipped out from under me. Arms flailing, I scrambled to regain my balance. Instead, I fell backwards, sucked into the creek's murky depths.

Chapter Four

A strong hand snagged my shirt collar, yanking my head out of the muddy water.

"What d'ya think yer doin'?" Mr. Hammond roared, his face red with fury.

Gasping for air, I struggled to stand. "Apples…." I choked. "I thought… the horses."

Mr. Hammond snatched the apples from my hand. "Mr. Slade told me you were just ridin' along. Didn't say nothin' 'bout babysittin' some fool child."

I hung my head. "I'm sorry."

"Come on, girls," Mr. Hammond said, holding the apples close to their nostrils. "Come get 'em."

The horses craned their necks, distracted by the sweet, juicy fruit. Clasping the harness tightly in his hand, Mr. Hammond took a couple of steps forward, crooning all the while. The horses followed, the wagon wobbling as it rolled through the swiftly flowing waters. A couple of times I held my breath as the cart tipped to one side, then righted itself.

Once we'd all made it safely to the other side, Mr. Hammond glanced my way. "Well, bully for you! Those apple slices done the trick."

I shrugged, then started trudging up the sodden bank, feet squelching in my boots. I knew he was trying to apologize for yelling at me, but I deserved it. I was a nuisance, a good-fer-nothin', just like Pa said.

The mud was so thick along the steep embankment, we had to stop every few seconds to knock off the gooey clumps sticking to the wheel spokes. Finally, we crested the bank, exhausted and ready for a break.

I flopped down on the grass, panting from the effort. Yanking off my filthy boots, I turned them upside down. Thick, brown water gushed out. My pants weren't much better, the hems caked with a thick coat of mud.

"Reckon now's a good time to eat," Mr. Hammond said, retrieving a basket from the wagon. "My wife Harriet, packs a good lunch."

While the horses carried us westward, we feasted on hard-boiled eggs, meat patties, thick slices of cornbread, and molasses cookies.

"How much further?" I asked, wiping crumbs from my mouth.

"Two, maybe three hours."

The landscape had changed noticeably on this side of Rush Creek. Instead of flat prairieland, we drove over rolling hills lush with buffalo grass. Golden Tickseed, aglow in their bright yellow petals and bright red centers, waved in the breeze. Wildflowers in beautiful shades of gold, blue, and purple grew lush across the fields. It felt like we'd crossed into another world.

Mr. Hammond removed a pinch of tobacco from his pouch, wedging it in one cheek.

"So, what happened after Slade told you no?" he asked, picking up where I'd left off.

I shifted my weight on the hard bench. I had skipped the part about my surname. That was my secret and secrets are best kept by one.

"The next morning, he sent for me," I told Mr. Hammond.

What I didn't tell him was how lucky I'd been to find that job. Tired of Pa's drinking and his violent moods, I had finally run away. Pa hadn't coped properly with Ma's death.

He turned that bitterness, that grief, that anger on me because I was a reminder that she died giving birth to me; as though it were my fault. When he started hitting me, I decided I'd had enough.

One night, I snuck out while he was sleeping, carrying little more than the clothes on my back, Ma's family Bible tucked in one of my shirts, and a spare set of clothes packed in a small carpetbag. I'd walked at night, sleeping in empty corn cribs or under stone bridges during the day.

After a week or so, I'd reached Julesburg where I was lucky enough to find Mr. Briggs' livery. A horse had stomped on his foot and broke it, so he hired me to help him out. His bad luck turned out to be my blessing.

"And?" Mr. Hammond prompted, bringing me back to my story.

"Asked if I still wanted to work for the Pony Express. I thought he'd changed his mind, so I said yes. He set a piece of paper on the table, told me to sign it. I tried to read it, but it was full 'a words I didn't know. Soon as I'd signed, he told me I was goin' to Mud Springs station to help out, that you was my ride, and I needed to meet ya at the General Store at dawn."

Mr. Hammond threw back his head and laughed. His laugh was as big and lusty as the rest of him. "He got ya good, didn't he? Mr. Slade's slicker than pig snot."

I could feel my cheeks grow warm. There wasn't anything funny about this. "I'm gonna show Mr. Slade how tough I am. Then he'll change his mind and hire me as a Pony Express rider."

Mr. Hammond let out another laugh, then coughed, choking on his tobacco. "Good luck with that."

Bending over the wheel, he spit out a stream of tobacco, then took a swig from a flask he kept hidden in his coat pocket.

"No need to tell anyone 'bout this either," he said, slipping it back into his pocket. "So that's how you found yourself hitchin' a ride with me," Mr. Hammond finished.

"Yes, sir."

"Jus' remember; Slade has a reputation. He can be rough and meaner 'n a bull if you get on his bad side. The scoundrel holds onto a grudge longer 'n a dog with a bone."

For a while, neither of us spoke, caught up in our own thoughts.

Abruptly, Mr. Hammond whipped out his rifle.

My heart skipped a beat. "What's the matter?"
Mr. Hammond nodded towards the horizon.
"Thought I saw somethin' movin',"
I glanced about, head whipping left and right, remembering the haunting howls of the wolves we'd heard this morning. What savage place was Mr. Slade sending me to?
Following the direction of his gaze, I spotted a blurry shape on the horizon, bearing down on us at an alarming speed.
Visions of outlaws, rustlers, and buffalo stampedes flooded my mind. I gulped. "What… what's that?"
"Not sure," Mr. Hammond mumbled.
The speck swelled to a dust cloud. All at once, Mr. Hammond's face relaxed. A smile creased his lips. "Jus' the Pony Express rider."
As it drew closer, the gray blur took on the form of horse and rider. I'd never seen such speed. The rider, laying low alongside the horse's back, appeared to be one with his steed as they flew across the fields. Onward they galloped, the pounding of hooves growing stronger and stronger as they came abreast, then whooshed by.
With an overpowering pang of envy, I watched the pair dwindle to a dark speck, then vanish over a hill. That should have been me.

Chapter Five

We crested a gentle swell about mid-afternoon, then dipped into a small vale. In the hollow of the bowl-shaped valley nestled a cluster of small, rundown buildings, Mud Springs station. Our wagon bumped and jounced down a dirt path worn bare by bare feet, shoes, boots, hoofs, horseshoes, wagon wheels, and coach wheels.

The buildings were simple structures, hastily built to function as one of the many relay stations along the Central Overland California and Pikes Peak Express Company route, also known as the Pony Express.

Sturdy, spacious, and over four times the size of the station house, the horse stables dwarfed all the other buildings. Behind the stables was a large corral where draft and quarter horses grazed alongside thoroughbreds.

The station house, on the other hand, was nothing more than a peat-roofed soddy with a low-cut door. A bushy crop of cress, pink asters, and purple morning-glories pushed through the soddy's sagging roof. When the wildflowers atop the house waved to and fro, in the breeze, the entire soddy looked as though it were swaying.

In the yard, a beautiful mare tethered to a hitching post chomped at the bit. Tossing her head as far as the tether allowed, ripples of silky black mane whipped about her strong, graceful neck. The spirited horse was stunning, with firm cords of muscle running along her powerful legs and broad shoulders.

Her thick black tail swished back and forth in quick, jerky movements of displeasure, irritating the man hunched low over her upturned hoof.

"Confound ya, Ebony!" the man hollered, giving her a look of annoyance. "Will ya please hold still?"

"Havin' trouble with the horses agin', Amos?" Mr. Hammond chuckled, reining in the horses.

The man dropped the hoof, stretched his back, then sauntered towards us. Muscles clenched and unclenched in his protruding jaw. Though I guessed him to be in his late thirties or forties, the weather had roughened his face. Deep lines crossed his broad forehead like furrows. He was built like a barrel, with wide shoulders, large thighs, muscular arms, and large, strong hands.

"Reckon Mr. Slade deliberately bought the most ornery, mean-spirited horses he could find," Amos griped, running a hand through his unruly mane of auburn hair.

Mr. Hammond dismounted. "Might be, but they sure can outrun anything. Ain't nothin' as fast as these thoroughbreds."

My legs almost buckled as I tried to stand, wobbly as a young calf's legs after the long ride.

Amos cast a fleeting glance my way. "This yer boy?"

"Nope, he's yer new helper. Mr. Slade hired him just yesterday in place of Tom."

"He... he what?" Amos bellowed, his face turning bright red as he glared at me. His eyes were cold and hard. "I need a man 'round here. Someone with some brawn. Not some sickly-looking waif Slade pulled from the gutter." He spit in the dirt.

I stood beside the cart for a moment, too stunned for words. Yet I was not one to shrink from a challenge. I pulled back my shoulders, stretching to my full height. "I ain't a kid. I'm almost fourteen." I'd added a year or two. Who was counting?

"Fourteen, eh?" Amos snorted.

He bent his large frame until we were eye to eye. I had to force myself not to look away. "Look, kid. This here's a hard job. I ain't gonna go soft on ya jus' 'cause yer small. If ya don't wanna break a sweat, ya better climb right back up in that wagon and go back to wherever ya came from. Got it?"

My first thought was to do as he suggested. Living in this wild land with some quarrelsome old coot didn't exactly excite me. But I wasn't a quitter. Besides, if I left now, I'd never get another chance to become a Pony Express rider.

Stepping away from Mr. Perkins, I marched back to the cart, head held high. I retrieved my bag, then turned to look at him.

"I'm stayin'," I said, trying to sound confident.

His eyes widened for a second, as though surprised by my words. Then his eyes narrowed. "Suit yerself." He spit out another frothy wad of spittle onto the ground. "You can start by unloadin' the cart."

Amos stormed off, leaving Mr. Hammond and me staring after him. Mr. Hammond gave me a sideways glance. "Friendly, ain't he?"

I fumbled with my sack, choking back tears. What I hadn't thought about was that, in my desperate hurry to flee one nightmare, I might have landed myself smack dab in the middle of another.

Mr. Hammond laid a hand on my shoulder. "Yer gonna be fine, boy. Amos may be a bit rough around the edges and won't hesitate to knock ya down a peg or two to remind ya who's boss. Jus' keep yer opinions to yerself and do as he asked."

He squeezed my shoulder then quickly dropped his hand as Amos led two fresh horses out of the barn. As soon as they were hitched to the wagon, Mr.

Hammond climbed into the driver's seat, flicked the reins, and drove off.

Despite my choice to stay, I felt a sense of regret as I watched the wagon clear the top of the hill, then disappear over the horizon. Mr. Hammond was the first grown up who had been kind to me. I just hoped I wouldn't regret my decision to stay at Mud Springs.

Chapter Six

The squat, rectangular soddy was nothing more than a shack, its walls built from strips of sod chopped into blocks two feet wide then stacked like overlapping bricks. Poles stretched from the front wall to the back wall, overlaid with layers of hay, dirt, and prairie grass. Boards that probably came from the dismantled wagon out in the yard had been nailed together to form a door.

The one-room dwelling was scarcely bigger than a train wagon and just as dark. Thin shafts of sunlight squeezed through two narrow slits cut into the front wall. They were like stockade loopholes which are primarily used to shoot at enemy forces. I hoped they weren't meant for that.

Pausing to let my eyes adjust to the gloom, I took a few moments to look around. The room was meagerly furnished with several overturned crates used as seating, set around a low table. The table was nothing more than two thin boards propped on a couple of barrels. Dirty dishes and candle stubs littered the tabletop.

Two narrow bunks had been wedged against the far wall. A large, shaggy buffalo robe covered the lower bunk. The top bunk sagged under a jumble of bags, jugs, crocks, and various tools.

A stove stood on the opposite side of the room, pots and cookware stacked willy-nilly beside it. A cast-iron stew pot sat on the stove top.

Over the door hung a variety of weapons; a long-barreled rifle, musket, powder horn, and a large axe. A clutter of tools, oilskins, and a pair of large boots lay in a heap near the door.

"So, ya like it?" Amos asked with a throaty laugh as he ducked through the doorway. But his laugh held no mirth. "Home sweet home."

With sudden dismay, I realized I was about to cry. I was supposed to be fourteen years old. Fourteen-year-olds don't cry. Ramming my hands into my pockets, I stormed out of the house.

"Nasty ol' coot," I muttered, scuffing my boots in the dirt.

Amos' voice carried through the open door. "When yer done puttin' the supplies away, muck out the barn."

I had a few ideas what I could do with the manure. Instead, I marched over to the stack of supplies and started lugging supplies into the soddy. It took several trips and, by the time I was done. I was worn out. Wiping a sleeve across my sticky brow, I stepped back out into the harsh sun and wandered over to what was left of an old, discarded wagon.

The salvaged wagon bed now served as a washing station with a basin, a cake of soap, and the ragged remnant of a gunny sack turned into a towel.

A metal dipper and tin cup, strung along the side of the wagon, rattled and clanged as a welcome breeze blew through the valley.

Unhooking the dipper, I plunged it into a nearby rain barrel, then poured the water over my head. The water wasn't as cold as I would have liked, but it was better than nothing. I dunked the dipper once more, drank the sun-warmed water, then ambled across the yard to the barn.

A passageway ran through the barn with six stalls on each side. On the near end was a tack room that smelled of leather oil. The cramped space was stocked with brushes, curry combs, blankets, twine, jars of grease, and hoof cream. Various tools lay strewn across a makeshift worktable.

Bridles and saddles hung on one wall. Among them were light weight saddles trimmed down to the basic horn, cantle, and stirrups. Pony Express riders used these, so the horses carried less weight, making them able to run faster. A mochila rested on the workbench. Two slits on the leather mochila fit over the fork and cantle with four pockets to hold the mail.

Grabbing the pitchfork propped against one of the walls, I headed down the passageway. A wheelbarrow had been left in front of a stall. Wheeling it over to the first stall, I stuck my head around the doorframe. The stall reeked of urine and manure. I tried to hold my breath as I stabbed the foul-smelling bedding with the pitchfork, then dumped it into the wheelbarrow.

Mucking out the stalls was hard. Over and over, I stabbed and tossed, stabbed and tossed, pitching soiled bedding into the wheelbarrow. Then I'd haul it out to the ever-growing manure heap.

After my fifth trip out to the dung pile, I took a moment to rest. My back was hurting as though someone had punched it hard. Knowing Amos was in the yard and couldn't see me back here, I leaned on my pitchfork, relishing a few minutes' idleness.

From here, I could watch the horses frolic in the corral. It was easy to spot the thoroughbreds from among the quarter horses. The quarter-horses were mild creatures, content to graze in the shade of the cottonwoods while Ebony and another black thoroughbred galloped around the enclosure in one continuous and fluid motion.

"One of these days I'm gonna ride ya, Ebony," I whispered, watching her toss her long, graceful neck as though shaking off invisible reins.

A loud, gruff voice bellowed, making me jump. "Hey kid, come gimme a hand."

"Confound it!" I groaned, propping the pitchfork against the wheelbarrow. "What does he want now?"

Wiping sweat from my brow, I hurried through the barn to the yard where Amos perched on a crate, head bent over the black mare's hoof.

"Hold her leg fer me," Amos barked.

I approached slowly to avoid spooking the mare. She was tall, towering well above my head. Her sleek, black coat shone in the golden sunlight and her thick, silky mane rippled across broad, muscular shoulders. She was more beautiful and more powerful than all the horses I'd cared for during my time at the livery.

I held out my hand. When she didn't shy away, I moved closer.

"Good girl," I crooned, stroking her soft fur. "Jus' hold still now."

Reaching into my pocket, I fished out the molasses cookie I'd saved from lunch. Though mostly crumbs by now, I held it in my palm, smiling as her big soft lips brushed against my hand, scooping up every morsel.

The horse nudged my hand, clearly asking for more. "Sorry, that's all I had," I said, scratching behind her ears.

Amos quickly set the shoe then rounded the toe. "Not sure how ya won 'er over but this is the first time she's held still since I started workin' on 'er. Jus' keep 'er distracted."

Once he was finished, Amos tossed the rasp on the ground and slowly eased his back straight again. "Put this beast back in the corral with the rest of them ornery brutes."

I scowled. She was not beast. I untied the mare, then led her to the corral. "He's the beast," I whispered in her ear.

I swung the gate open, smiling as she sped away, her beautiful mane whipping like a flag in the breeze, long muscles rippling under an inky black coat. Her movements were graceful, well-controlled, her bearing regal. Leaning against the fence, I watched, spellbound.

"Ya gonna stand there gawkin' all day?" Amos shouted. He ran a dirty hand across his forehead, leaving a dark streak on his brow.

"I ain't ...," I began, but Amos was already walking away.

Glaring at his back, I kicked a pebble, sending it skittering across the yard.

"Do this, do that," I muttered, stomping back to the barn. Snatching up the pitchfork, I jabbed it deep into a heap of soiled straw. "No wonder Tom left. Man's ornery than a rattlesnake in the summer sun."

Chapter Seven

It had grown dusky by the time I wrapped up my chores. I hobbled across the yard on sore, tired feet, my eyelids drooping with exhaustion. Every part of me ached.

The stench of burnt food hit me as I stumbled through the door.

"Grab a plate and help yerself," Amos mumbled from the table where he sat, chewing on an antelope rib. He bit off another large chunk of meat, grease dribbling down his chin.

Glancing into the cast-iron pan, I found a greasy hunk of meat resting atop charred beans. Hoping it tasted better than it looked, I scooped up a small serving, then plopped down on a crate. My stomach lurched as I stared at the foul-smelling glob of beans in front of me.

"What's the matter? Not fond of my cookin'?" Amos said, biting off another chunk of meat. "Just eat your food and be thankful you ain't going to bed hungry."

I glanced up. He was watching me, his gaze scornful. This wasn't about the food but a test of my character.

I lifted the spoon, my stomach balking at the thought of eating the disgusting food. The beans had barely touched my lips when I felt the urge to throw up. Hoping to wash away the terrible taste, I snatched up the pot of coffee and poured some in a cup. Out came a strong dark brew. I took a sip, then leaned over and spit it out on the ground.

"This stuff ain't drinkable."

"Go thirsty, then." Amos shrugged, reaching for his own cup.

The mug was halfway to his lips when he froze. The room went still as he stared at the top of my head. His gaze was fixed, unblinking, like a cat stalking its prey. The hairs on the back of my neck prickled. I was staring into the face of a predator.

Terrified, I started to rise, ready to flee. This man was crazy.

"Don't... move!" Amos hissed.

I froze, my mind yelling. "*Run! Run before he kills you.*" Yet my feet wouldn't budge. A soft moan squeezed through my lips.

Amos set his cup on the table; his movements unhurried as he reached for the long, sharp knife lying next to his plate. Grease dripped from the steel blade. Gripping the dagger firmly in his large hand, Amos raised it above his head then gradually rose to his feet.

Don't scream, don't scream, I thought even as I opened my mouth to scream. Amos advanced, every step slow and deliberate. Eyes wide with fear, I watched as he approached.

The man's crazy. He's going to stab you. Run while you can.

"Don't... move," Amos repeated. He stood motionless, just staring at me.

He's going to kill me. He's going to kill me then bury my body. I whimpered. In that second of shear panic, I wondered if that's what happened to Tom. Had Amos killed him just like he was going to kill me, then buried the body in some secluded place?

With a sudden burst of speed, the big man pounced. Flinging myself to my knees, I let out a scream. Out of the corner of my eye, I saw Amos thrust the knife downward. Throwing my hands over my head, I curled into a ball, squeezed my eyes shut, then waited for the fierce burn as the knife sliced into my back.

I heard a loud *'thwack!'* crumpled to the floor, my body limp as a rag doll. I laid still for several seconds, unable to move, unable to breathe. My lungs felt like they were bursting.

"Well, I'll be!" A burst of hysterical laughter filled the room. "If this ain't the biggest scorpion I ever seen."

Cautiously, like a turtle peering out of its half open shell, I glanced up. Skewered to the wall, a mere inch from where my head had been seconds ago, was a scorpion the size of a chicken egg.

Amos yanked the knife out of the wall, his gaze following the scorpion as it dropped to the floor. Calmly, he wiped the blade on his shirt, thrust the dagger into the tabletop, then went back to his meal as though nothing had happened.

I was shaking so badly; I could barely stand. Suddenly, I began to heave. Stumbling to the door, I rushed out, spewing my lunch on the ground. I was still heaving when Amos sauntered past.

"Come on, kid. Time to see to the horses."

I wiped my mouth on my sleeve then staggered after him.

Chapter Eight

We bedded down the horses, pitching fresh hay into their feeders, then giving them each a scoop of grain. Then, Amos called me into the tack room.

"These saddles are smaller 'n lighter than the regular saddles. They're made 'specially fer the Pony Express. Make sure ya keep 'em separate from the regular saddles."

He moved to a far wall where a map hung next to a schedule.

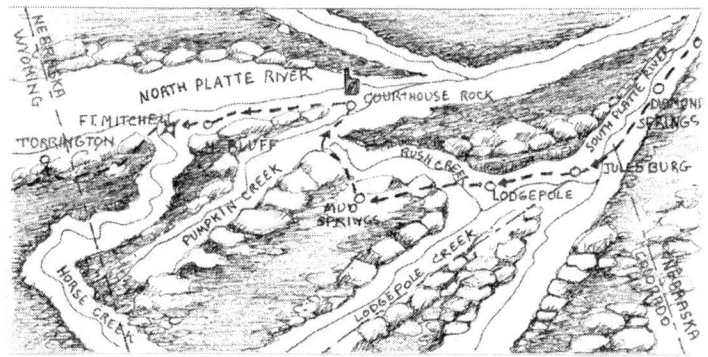

"This here's a map of the Pony Express route. This other one lists the riders' schedules. It's important to remember the times 'cause we need to have a fresh mount waitin' when they ride into our station. Sometimes the riders run late. Bad weather, hurt horse.... Whatever, ya still gotta be ready. Don't mess it up. I ain't got no patience for mistakes."

I glanced at the map, stifling a yawn.

"Right... then, get some sleep," Amos said. "We got us a busy day tomorrow."

As we stepped from the barn, Amos glanced at the dark, heavy sky. He sniffed the air then shook his head. "Storm's brewin'."

I was thankful I wouldn't be sleeping under the stars tonight. I'd been caught in a couple of rainstorms in the days following my escape. I'd quickly discovered there's nothing quite as miserable as sleeping under a damp, cold, stone bridge.

I followed Amos back into the soddy. The smell of burnt beans mixed with bitter coffee made me queasy.

"Where ya want me to sleep?" I said, as Amos dropped onto the lower bunk.

"If ya wanna sleep on the top bunk, yer gonna have to move all the stuff," he mumbled, unlacing his boots. "Jus' make sure ya put it in a dry place and cover it with an oil cloth."

He tugged his boots off, shoving them under the bed.

I glanced at the top bunk stacked high with supplies. I was to weary to mess with it. "Can I... can I sleep in the barn for now?"

"Suit yerself," Amos mumbled, waving a hand dismissively. "Jus' make sure ya don't keep the horses up all night." He chuckled but it came out sounding like a snort.

Rolling my eyes, I grabbed my bag and escaped into the murky night. Halfway to the barn I paused, breathing in lungfuls of fresh air. All around me were hills. In the twilight, they no longer looked like individual hills. One hill rose, then fell only to rise again in the shape of another hill, undulating like a giant serpent across the horizon.

Dark clouds, hanging low over the western hills, scampered across the sky, cloaking the moon. Darkness filled the valley. The storm Amos had mentioned was closing in. Wishing I hadn't lingered so long, I stumbled across the yard, startled into a sprint as a flash of lightning zipped across the sky.

Thunder boomed. I reached the stables just as the first, fat raindrops pelted the ground. Standing just inside the door, I watched another fierce bolt slash the night sky. Seconds later, thunder boomed, rattling the barn with enough force to set my heart pounding. One of the horses let out a squeal, kicking the walls of its stall in fright.

Retreating further inside, I slammed the door closed. In the darkness, I paused to get my bearings. The smell of straw, animals, and leather were familiar and comforting to me. They reminded me of the livery and my bed in the loft above the stalls where I'd slept during the time I'd worked there.

Using fingers and toes to guide me, I felt my way to one of the empty stalls. I grabbed a blanket that hung over the half door and spread it on the straw. With only my thin jacket to cover me, I nestled in, cringing as my sore, tired muscles complained about the day's grueling work.

For a while I laid still, growing accustomed to my new surroundings. Outside, the wind howled, shaking the barn walls. Rain lashed at the roof. A boom of thunder made me jump. In their stalls, the horses snorted and stomped, terrified by the fierce storm.

I couldn't sleep with all the noise. Instead, I thought about Amos. A feeling of worry churned in my stomach. He was a hard man, and I hoped my time with him wouldn't come to a bad end. My thoughts then turned to Pa. What would he be up to right now? Would he be looking for me or was he relieved not to have me in the way?

I say *home*, but Pa hardly made our house feel like a home. He never cleaned the place nor raised a hand to help with meals or laundry. Meals mostly consisted of porridge or mush, or whatever vegetables he snatched from someone's garden.

I eventually took to spying on our neighbor through her kitchen window, watching as she sliced, diced, mixed, poured, and plucked, creating mouth-watering meals. I would copy down everything she prepared, jotting notes in the margins of the Daily Bill newspaper. I'd run home and try to repeat whatever she'd made that day, swapping some of the ingredients with whatever we had around the house.

I kept hoping Pa would change, but as the years went by, he only grew worse. The day I fled, I promised myself I would never go back. I was done with Pa, done with my past. I was an orphan. My life was my own now. I just hoped I wouldn't mess it up.

Chapter Nine

Dawn came much too soon. I awoke to the sound of rain drumming on the roof. For a moment, I thought I was at Mr. Brigg's and briefly wondered if Ms. Briggs had finally cooked that obnoxious rooster that woke me every morning before the sun had even stirred.

The memory of yesterday's journey rushed back to me. I was no longer in Julesburg. I was out in the middle of nowhere, on some secluded station, with some crazy man.

I didn't want to get up just yet but needed to go to the bathroom. Reluctantly, I half rose, then eased back onto the hay when pain shot through my back and limbs. I pushed myself into a sitting position, back against the wall.

After a few minutes, I rolled onto my knees, stood, using the half door for support. Brushing bits of hay from my pants and shirt, I hobbled down the passageway.

It was a damp and cheerless morning that greeted me as I pulled the barn door open. The relentless rain had turned the yard into a sea of mud. Taking a deep breath, I tucked my pants into my boots, pulled my coat tighter around my neck and stepped into the downpour. Head lowered against the driving rain, I slogged through inches of slippery mud.

"I hate this place!" I grumbled, as I slipped and fell to one knee. Cold, muddy water seeped into my boot, soaking my pants. Tears smarted behind my eyes. Swallowing hard, I pushed myself to my feet, willing the tears away. *Stop yer cryin',* I scolded myself. *Yer better than this.*

After relieving myself, I stumbled across the yard. By the time I reached the soddy, I was soaking wet. I'd hoped to find a warm dry house with breakfast on the stove. Instead, I found a cold, wet house.

It was raining inside, almost as much as it was outside. Raindrops trickled steadily through the peat roof, plinking into buckets, pots, cups, jars, tin cans, an old boot, or whatever was on hand. The air was thick with the smell of damp earth.

Amos threw me a withering look as I stumbled through the door.

"Roof leaks like a sieve," he grumbled from the table where he sat, slouched over a cup of coffee. Dark shadows circled his eyes. Amos waved a hand in the direction of the stove. "There's left-overs in the pot if yer hungry."

Skirting an assortment of pots, I weaved my way across the room. I cast a quick glance into the pot. A cold, slimy slab of lard nearly an inch thick lay atop the beans. Yuk!

If he thinks I'm gonna eat this, he's wrong. Casting about for something else to eat, my gaze fell on the supplies crowding the top bunk. Side-stepping puddles and pots, I rummaged through the bags under the oilcloth.

I found a sack of cornmeal, a bag of salt, along with a jug of maple syrup. Arms full, I woven my way back to the table and set the ingredients on the only dry space, between two tin buckets that were nearly overflowing.

"Don't go wastin' my supplies now, ya hear?" Amos griped.

"I ain't wastin' yer supplies," I snapped. "I ain't too sure how you work things out here, but from where I come, ya give a man a decent breakfast if ya want 'im to put in a decent day's work."

I regretted the words the second they came out of my mouth. I prepared myself for an outburst, yet, Amos didn't say a word, just looked at me with the same measured look he'd given me when I'd first arrived.

I turned away, focusing my attention on tending the stove. The fire had gone out without even one tiny ember among the logs to help revive it. I filled the stove with firewood, then, lit some kindling to speed it along. The logs were so damp, it was a struggle to get the flames to take hold.

Eventually, I heard the satisfying crackle. I grabbed one of the pans set out to catch raindrops, then, dumped the muddy water outside, filling it with clean water from the rain barrel.

Setting the pan on the stove, I watched until tiny bubbles began to dance across the surface, then added a cupful of cornmeal and a dash of salt. With a wooden spoon, I stirred the cornmeal mush until it turned thick and creamy.

An unusual noise came from the room behind me, a deep growl that made the hairs on the back of my neck prickle. What wild creature had crept into the house? Shaking from head to toe, I snatched up a cast iron skillet, lifted it over my head, then spun around.

There was no bear. There was no mountain lion. Just Amos, one side of his face smooshed against the table, sound asleep. Loud raspy snores mingled with dark drool escaped from slightly parted lips. Of all the fool things! For half a second, I was tempted to slam the pan down on the table right next to his head and startle him awake.

Instead, I sank onto one of the upturned crates, trying to steady my nerves. Amos' loud snuffles and snorts, mixed with the maddening *plink, plink, plop* of raindrops, made me glad I'd chosen to sleep in the barn.

With a loud sigh, I went back to work, wiping crumbs off the table, scraping up patches of hardened wax where candles had spilled over. I heated coffee on the stove, filled two plates with cornmeal mush, then, slapped Amos' plate down on the table inches from his nose.

Amos bolted upright. "Who... what?" He stammered. his eyes wide with surprise.

"Eat up," I said. Ooh, that felt so good!

Amos glanced down at his bowl. "What's this?"

"Cornmeal," I said, pouring warm maple syrup onto his mush. I planted myself on one of the crates, watching as he picked up his spoon, took a bite, then tucked in with gusto.

"What d'ya think?" I asked.

"Had better," he muttered, washing down his last mouthful with a gulp of coffee. With a loud burp, he pushed his plate away. "Better git the day started."

He stood and pulled on his raincoat. "Once you're done …."

His words were cut short as part of the roof fell in, showering clumps of mud and wet grass onto the table. A slippery, black coil tumbled through the hole and landed right in front of me.

I jumped up so fast, I knocked over my seat. The snake uncurled, slid across the table, then dropped to the ground. Quick as a whip, Amos stooped, clutched the snake behind its head, yanked open the door, then, tossed it into the yard.

"Find somethin' to put under that hole, will ya?" Amos said as he shoved a ratty hat on his head. "It's lettin' in the rain."

Spinning on his heel, he ducked out into the soggy morning, slamming the door behind him.

Chapter Ten

The skies had opened wide while we'd been eating breakfast, a fierce and steady rain that quickly flooded our little valley. Saddled and ready, Dash waited patiently beside me for the Pony Express rider. Amos had conveniently found something to do in the tack room while I was given the task of lookout. Every few seconds, a strong gust of wind blew the rain sideways, drenching me as I stood in the doorway, listening for hoofbeats.

The minutes stretched on. Still, I stood my post, reluctant to show any sign of weakness. If Amos wanted to test my mettle, I'd show him I had plenty of grit.

Suddenly, an eerie howl echoed from the hills.

A-ooooow, a-ooooow!

My blood ran cold as Amos hurried from the tack room. "Is… is that… ?" I stammered.

Amos snorted loudly. "That's jus' Clyde, warnin' us he's comin'."

I stared out at the rain, feeling like a fool.

"Well, don't jus' stand there like a dolt," Amos said, shaking his head.

Yanking the reins from my hand, he led the mare out into the yard. I clenched my fists, following, mud squishing underfoot, sucking at my boots, making each step a struggle.

Horse and rider thundered into the station, spraying mud left and right. Despite the hat pulled over his brow, I had a feeling I'd seen this man before. The ginger curls under his droopy hat were a dead give-away. By golly, it was the cocky young rider I'd bumped into at the boarding house! Today, he looked more like a drowned rat with his shaggy curls hanging limply around his face, wet clothes clinging tightly to his slender body.

"Hey there, Clyde. Best be careful of Rush Creek," Amos warned as the rider slid off his horse, retrieved the mochila, then tossed it over Dash's saddle. "Heard it's pretty high, even at the pass."

"Will do."

Amos released Dash's reins then backed away as Clyde leapt into the saddle. Pulling the horse's head about, Clyde dashed off as quickly as he had come, Dash's hooves spurting mud in her wake.

I was standing much too close. Mud spurted up into my face and down the front of me. Amos doubled over, howling with laughter.

"Ya got a lot to learn, kid," Amos whooped, as he led the horse to be curried. "First lesson is, stand clear or mud spurts right up into your face. Unless ya want a mud bath, that is."

I was furious. I was humiliated. I wanted nothing more than to leave this hateful place, this hateful man, this hateful job. I hated the way he treated me like a little child, hated the way he made me feel like an idiot. I just wanted to – I wasn't sure what I wanted to do, but I would think of something.

Turning my back on him, I wiped my face with my sleeve, then spit dirt from my mouth. Then and there, I decided to learn everything I could so I'd become the best station worker in the Overland California and Pikes Peak Express Company.

One of these days, Mr. Slade would notice my hard work and decide I'd earned the right to be one of his riders. *Go ahead and laugh Amos,* I thought, 'cause *one of these days I'll be laughing at you.*

"Grab one 'a them empty feed sacks and rub 'im down," Amos barked as I entered the barn.

The poor steed was about done in; his flanks were heaving, the muscles in his neck quivering dangerously fast. His nostrils were dilated from a grueling run and it showed in every part of his body.

Removing the saddle, I started rubbing him down, moving gradually down along its withers, its flanks, and haunches. I was concentrating so hard on my task, I didn't even notice the bucket of water Amos had just set down. Taking another step to the right, my foot plunged into the bucket.

Tumbling sideways, I tried to grab the horse to stop myself from falling. Surprised, Thunder kicked out, planting a foot right in my gut, sending me flying clear across the barn.

Wham!

Slamming into the far wall, I slid down onto a heap of soiled straw. A burst of laughter filled the barn. "Gotta pay more attention kid. Didn't ya see the bucket?"

"No, I didn't," I snapped.

Clasping my belly, I winced. "It ain't funny, either."

I was tempted to snatch up the empty bucket and hurl it at Amos' head. Instead, I flung it across the barn, rose to my feet, then stormed out.

Chapter Eleven

I stayed inside the rest of that day. I thought it better to stay out of sight to give us both time for tempers to cool. I emptied the pots, then set them out again to catch the drips which seemed to be multiplying faster than rabbits in the springtime.

I spent the morning cleaning up the stack of dishes piled on the table. Lugging clean water from the rain barrel, I heated it on the stove then poured it into the dishpan. After searching for several minutes, I finally found a cake of soap under a stack of rags. Grease stuck to the plates so I had to scrub hard. By the time I was done, my arms were aching.

Then I sorted through the supplies on the top bunk. We didn't have much to work with. Without cows or chickens, we had no eggs, no milk, and no cheese. Maybe once it stopped raining, I could do a little hunting. I'd learned how to snare rabbits so maybe I'd try catching a wild turkey, a prairie chicken, or a guinea hen.

I could go exploring too. If I was lucky, I might come upon a wild fowl's nest. My mouth watered at the thought of scrambled eggs. Morel mushrooms, those cone-shaped bits of deliciousness, would soon be ready to pick. Wild berries, plums, apples, and nuts might also grow nearby. I'd have to ask Amos.

Then I started to work on dinner. I poured the leftover cornmeal mush into a hot pan, then waited for the mush to harden. Once it was firm, I poured it onto a plate, mixed it well, then formed small cake-like patties called Johnny cakes. I cooked them up in a frying-pan greased with pork-rind, along with a few strips of cured bacon,

It was almost dark when Amos finally came in from his chores. We ate in brooding silence, huddled over our plates, wearing oil cloths against the raindrops. We made a miserable pair.

A headache had been steadily building behind my eyes. I rubbed my temples, closing my eyes for a couple of seconds, then rolled my neck to stretch out the stiffness. When I opened my eyes, I noticed Amos was staring at me. He had a strange look on his face.

"What? Don't tell me there's another scorpion?" I yelped, ready to bolt.

Amos shook his head then dropped his gaze. "Nothin'," he mumbled. "It's jus' that... well, fer a minute there, ya reminded me of someone I once knew."

Were those tears I saw in his eyes? They couldn't be. Amos had no heart; therefore he couldn't feel sadness, right? I shrugged it off as a trick of the candlelight then bit into another Johnny Cake. They had turned out well considering the little I had to work with.

Amos pushed his empty plate aside then let out a loud burp. Snatching up the *St. Joseph Gazette* Mr. Hammond had delivered along with the supplies, Amos slid it across the table.

"Read the important stuff to me while I oil my boots," he said, unlacing his right boot.

Grudgingly, I picked up the newspaper, unfolded it, then ran through the bold-lettered captions. The news was mostly about some man named Abraham Lincoln.

"Abraham Lincoln has won the Repu… bli… can nom…ina…. tion," I read, stumbling over the long, unfamiliar words.

Amos slammed his hand on the table so hard, I nearly toppled off my seat. The lantern teetered dangerously. I grabbed it and set it straight again.

"Finally, some good news!" he said.

"Why was that?" I asked. I didn't know a whole lot about politics.

"'cause Lincoln's against slavery," Amos said. "But his opponent, Mr. Douglas, don't care one bit 'bout them poor black folks."

Amos picked up a cloth, poured oil on it, then started rubbing it onto one of his boots. "Funny thing is, if Lincoln wins, it'll be another slap in the face fer his rival."

"How come?"

"'cause Lincoln married the gal Douglas was courtin'. What else is in the paper?"

I picked up where I'd left off. "As a young man, Lincoln earned money by spittin' hogs."

I knew it had come out wrong as soon as the words spilled from my mouth and felt warmth rise to my cheeks. Head down, I pressed out the wrinkles in the paper as though by doing so I could erase those last two words.

Amos dropped his boot on the floor and let out a howl of laughter.

"Splittin' logs," I corrected, feeling like a bumbling idiot once again.

"Think ya better git some sleep," Amos said, wiping tears of laughter from his eyes.

Tossing the paper back onto the table, I grabbed my jacket then scampered out into the pouring rain. Without moonlight to guide me, I had to inch my way across the yard, feeling with the tip of my boots for rocks or pools of water. Luckily, I managed to reach the barn without any trouble.

Removing my wet clothes, I draped them over one of the stall doors to dry, then sank onto the straw. A deep feeling of loneliness wrapped around me like a blanket. I was no stranger to loneliness; I'd always been on my own, even when Pa had been home.

Usually, he'd ignore me.

Sometimes he'd cuss me out enough to send me fleeing out to the barn. Yet here, with miles of emptiness between stations, I felt the enormity of my loneliness more than ever. It was obvious Amos didn't want me around. I'd been a fool for coming here, hoping life would be better than at home.

I began to cry. I cried for the mother I wished I'd known. I cried for all that could have been if she'd lived. I cried for all those years of loneliness. Then in the darkness, I heard a soft whinny.

I sat up and dried my tears, listening in the darkness. Another gentle whinny drew me to my feet. The sound was coming from next door. I made my way towards the stall to my right. Ebony nickered, thrusting her head over the half door.

"Hey there, Ebony," I whispered, stroking her forehead.

Ebony whickered and lowered her massive head onto my shoulder.

"You know I'm sad, don't you?"

The mare nuzzled my neck and I was comforted. For a while, we kept company, my arms wrapped around Ebony's strong neck, her head resting softly against mine.

"Thank you, Ebony," I said, when I finally pulled away. "Thank you for being my friend."

I patted her neck, scratched behind her ears, then returned to my bed. I lay silently, listening to the soft sounds of snuffling, grunting, and contented chewing. One of the horses rattled its food dish, likely trying to lick up the last morsels of grain.

I scrunched up in the straw and sighed. With Ebony for a friend, I would never truly be lonely.

Chapter Twelve

The barn became my shelter, the one place where I could relax and be myself. Ebony was a good listener, ears perked as I griped about the weather and the endless chores. Mostly, I grumbled about Amos.

"Muck out the stalls, haul firewood, lug more buckets of water from the springs, clean my clothes, cook the meals, wash the dishes," I vented to her one day. "This ain't a happy place to work, that's for sure."

Amos was a surly man, grumpy, moody, prickly as a briar patch. He seemed to resent my presence, doing his best to make me feel like an intruder. I felt unwelcome, unwanted, unappreciated.

He hovered like a hawk, watching, scowling, griping, complaining, badgering, and finding fault with everything I did. It wasn't unusual for him to belittled me or start a quarrel over some silly little detail. When I tried to be friendly or ask him questions, his answers were short and snippy.

Occasionally, a wagon party heading west or a stagecoach carrying passengers passed through. Most often our tiny station was merely a chance for stagecoaches to switch out horses while grabbing a bite to eat before moving on.

Sometimes they broke their long journey at our station, staying overnight. Amos would stay busy in the barn until they left again, leaving me to cook, feed them supper, cook their breakfast, and clean up after them.

The lousy weather didn't help much, either. Since I'd arrived, all it had done was rain, rain, rain. The station was living up to its name, the mud puddles growing and multiplying till the whole yard was a huge mire of brown, gooey muck. Everywhere I went, I saw nothing but brown, dull, boring brown; the yard, the soddy, the barn, the muddy springs. Even the hares, the deer, and the raccoons were that same drab brown.

Yet despite of the tough work and wretched living conditions, I always felt a thrill seeing the Pony

Express riders sprint into the station, switch horses, then gallop away within a five to ten seconds timespan.

Clyde and Miller, two riders responsible for our section of the route, ran the mail from Julesburg to Scott's Bluff. They would stay at their home stations on both ends of the route until the next batch of mail was ready for delivery.

Every few days they whipped through, thundering into the station as though a tornado were riding on their heels. I barely had time to run into the yard as they switched horses, exchanged a hurried greeting with Amos, then dashed off again. Lingering for a few seconds, I watched enviously as the riders grew smaller, then vanished over the hill. Those brief moments were the highlight of my days.

One of these days, I'll be the one on the horse, I kept reminding myself. *Jus' keep waiting, work hard, and hope for the best.*

Mr. Slade passed through several weeks after I'd arrived. As soon as I stepped out to grab his horse, his face broke into a smile.

"Well, if it isn't Mr. Barber!" he'd said, handing over the reins. "How do you like your job so far?"

"Well, sir," I said, hesitantly. "It's okay. But I'd still rather be a rider."

"I'll keep that in mind," Mr. Slade said, setting his large hand on my shoulder.

Just then, Amos emerged from the stables. "Hello, Mr. Slade!" he said, amiably. "What brings ya to our neck of the woods?"

"Jus' passin' through on my way to Scott's Bluff. Figured I'd get me a fresh mount."

Amos signaled me to take Mr. Slade's horse into the barn. "I'll get one saddled fer ya right quick."

"How the lad workin' out fer you?" Mr. Slade asked, as I started to lead his horse away.

"He can be a bit thick at times, but he'll do. For now, at least," Amos replied, loud enough that I heard him.

"Lad says he wants to become a rider."

Amos snorted. "He has no idea what he's talkin' 'bout."

I shouldn't have been surprised by his comments yet they hurt nonetheless. As a result, I ended up sulking all day.

When I finally went to bed, I laid awake for a while, imagining myself in the place of Clyde or Miller. In this fantasy, I would ride high and proud upon Ebony's back, looking down upon a mud-spattered Amos, before dashing off into the horizon. This daydream never failed to bring a smile to my face.

Eventually the rain let up. Our muddy valley turned bone dry. Amos decided to mend the leaky roof. After gathering several wheel-barrows full of mud and hay, we removed what was left of the roof, replacing it with a thick coat of mud mixed with brush and grass. Amos mixed a mud plaster which I used to fill the chinks.

Amos tamped it down with his big, strong hands. Finally, we sprinkled a layer of coarse gravel over the finished roof to prevent gusts of wind from blowing the brush and grass away. The new roof was sturdy enough to stand up to heavy rain.

Once the roof was done, we started on the walls, filling the holes with patches of sod and mud plaster. Then we sprinkled clay blended with coal oil over the walls to lessen the amount of dust in the house. Hopefully, this would mean less time spent cleaning.

A couple of months after I'd arrived at Mud Springs, I had my biggest argument with Amos. A glorious sun woke me that morning, the chinks in the barn walls letting in a spill of light.

"See to the horses. They need to be outside 'stead of the hot barn," Amos barked as soon as I stepped through the door of the soddy.

He appeared to be in one of his foul moods. I knew better than to argue with him. If he wanted to wait until later to eat breakfast, so be it.

I hurried across the yard, into the barn. The horses were shuffling their feet, eager to enjoy the sunshine.

"Okay, okay. I know it's a gorgeous day. Just give me a minute."

I released the horses one at a time, making my way from the back end of the stables to the front. Thunder, being his usual ornery self, was stomping and snorting, causing a ruckus.

"Calm down," I said, sliding the bolt on his gate open. I slipped into his stall. "I didn't forget ya."

Thunder tossed his head.

"I know you're upset. Now move over." I was trying to squeeze past his rump to untie his lead but he wasn't having it. He let out a loud snort, raised his back leg, then brought it down hard on my foot.

I gasped, winded as hot pain shot down to my toes and up my leg. "Get off my foot, you big brute!" I yelled, jabbing his rump hard with my elbow.

Thunder shuffled sideways then shook his head.

"You big, ol' bully," I said, hobbling as I led Thunder outside.

Thankfully, he was the last one to be released. I fastened the corral gate, then eased myself to the ground behind the barn. Gingerly, I removed my boot.

"Ooh, that 'urts." I wiggled my toes. They didn't look broken.

The bridge of my foot looked the worst with a bright red mark arching across the top. I didn't think my foot was broken but it hurt to stand it.

I propped my foot on my boot then closed my eyes for a moment, enjoying the early-morning breeze blowing through the valley. Before I knew it, I was asleep.

A deep, booming voice jolted me awake.

"Foolin' 'round behind my back, are ya?" Amos yelled as he towered over me. His face was dark with fury.

I jumped to my feet, then let out a strangled cry as a shock of pain seared through my foot.

"Ain't foolin' 'round," I protested. "Thunder stomped on my foot. Look at …."

Amos cut me off. "Well suck it up, boy."

Grabbing my arm, he squeezed it hard. His face was so close, I could smell coffee on his breath.

"This here's a hard job. Ya can't jus' stop 'cause ya got scuffed up a bit. Tough it out or git out."

"I… I…," I started, then stopped. It was no use arguing with him.

I shrugged his hand off then turned away. Amos stormed off and within seconds, the *slam-whoosh, slam-whoosh* of his axe could be heard. In between blows of his axe, I heard him grumbling.

Frustration bubbled up inside me as I picked up my boot and gingerly slipped it on. My foot had already begun to swell and throbbed inside the boot. As the pain took hold, frustration turned to anger and something inside of me snapped. I'd had it with Amos. If he was so tough, then he could take care of Mud Springs station all by himself.

Rounding the barn, I saw him wielding his axe with terrifying force. *Slam-whoosh.* Two log halves went soaring across the yard in opposite directions.

I hobbled into the barn, snatched my carpetbag, and started throwing my belongings inside. The more I thought about the way he treated me, the angrier I grew.

"I hate 'im, hate 'im," I raged. Grabbing a shirt, I crammed it into the bag. "Hate 'im, hate this job, hate everythin' about this stupid place!"

Bag over one shoulder, I limped out of the barn, into bright sunlight. Tears flooded my eyes, blurring the path ahead. I brushed them away impatiently, fighting the pain as I stumbled up the hill. At the top, I looked around. There was nothing but empty, desolate land as far as my eyes could see.

The reality of my situation hit me like a punch to the gut. At best, it would take me several days to reach the nearest neighbor and that was with two good feet. My injured foot would slow me down quite a bit. There were the wolves and coyotes who might possibly track me down and have me for dinner.

I had to face the truth; I was alone with some hateful man, out in the middle of nowhere. Other than the occasional traveler passing through, I had little contact with the rest of the world. I was stuck in this hateful place until Mr. Hammond or some other kindly soul offered me a ride out of here. I would go… where would I go? I had no idea, but would figure it out along the way.

Flinging my bag on the ground, I threw myself down beside it and let the tears flow. Why was Amos so hard to live with? Why did he dislike me? What had I ever done to make him mad at me? Was it me or my lack of experience that made him belittle me all the time?

Deep down, I knew I had to go back; back to hateful Amos, back to the filth and drudgery, back to working dawn to dusk for someone who didn't even like me.

In the meantime, I had to stay here. I had no other choice. I was still hoping Mr. Slade would notice I would make a good rider. Then I could turn my back forever on Amos and this miserable mudhole.

Knowing, however, was a whole lot easier than doing. Gritting my teeth, I pushed myself back on my feet, picked up my bag, then hobbled back down the hill. Chin held high, I limped across the yard and into the barn.

Not once did Amos glance my way.

Chapter Thirteen

The rainy spring eventually passed. Now a sultry summer was setting in. Our valley turned into a dry, dusty bowl. My main chore was to keep the rain barrel and watering troughs full. Hauling water was hot, grueling work. All too soon I found myself wishing it would rain again.

The soddy, with its thick walls and lack of sunlight, stayed cool despite the sweltering heat. It became home to snakes, mice, and other rodents who burrowed into the walls to escape the stifling weather. Field roaches, beetles, grasshoppers, and locusts crawled in through gaps or holes, nestling into pots, boots, clothes piles, bunks, or wherever they could find a cool dark place to sleep.

The springs, protected from the harsh sun by a curtain of trees, also provided a break from the sticky heat. Bucket in hand, I would run down the hill then jump into the cool, refreshing water, clothes and all. A quick dip to rinse off the sweat was the highpoint of those long, hot summer days.

If Amos was off hunting or caught up in some time-consuming chore, I grabbed the chance to spend a little extra time in the water, dunking my head underwater to blow bubbles with the minnows or digging for lizards hiding in the pool's muddy floor.

With the summer heat, the barn had grown too stuffy. I lugged a blanket down to the springs each night, spreading it on the soft mossy ground beneath the old weeping willow overhanging the water. I felt snug and happy in my cool leafy haven, dozing off to the chirping of crickets or rustling leaves whispering gently in the night breeze.

One evening, I was startled by some creature calling *who, who, who* in the darkening gloom. Glancing up, I spotted a large brown owl. Perched in the old oak tree, he stared down at me with a fierce scowl, his eyes round and yellow as egg yolks. Thick white eyebrows, a sharp hooked beak, a pair of ears, pointed straight up like untidy tufts of hair, and mottled black and brown plumage completed his sober-eyed, no-nonsense look which reminded me so much of Amos.

"Who?" I said, winking, then laughed when he winked back.

For several evenings in a row, the owl returned to the oak tree. I knew he was looking for supper, yet I told myself he was coming to see me. I taunted him with a barrage of who's until he grew tired of my antics and turned his head backwards in dismissal. I missed him terribly when he eventually stopped coming to the springs.

Most days, I woke at daybreak. In the soft light of dawn, I drowsily watched as gophers or raccoons ventured down to the pools to drink. Sometimes, a deer or a rabbit peered cautiously from the safety of a nearby thicket, twitching its little nose to sniff the air, before slinking down to the water's edge.

In the branches above, Meadowlarks perched, their bright yellow chests puffing out as they warbled their morning greetings. Though they never let me approach, these early-morning visitors grew used to my presence and no longer shied away.

One sultry day, I spotted a large cloud of dust on the horizon. Squinting, I could just make out several pale brown humps plodding along in the noontime heat. At first, I thought it might be a herd of buffalo. Buffalos could do a lot of damage to our station if they were startled and broke into a stampede. I was about to run and warn Amos when I realized the dust cloud snaking its way down the eastern hill, was a caravan of covered wagons. It was headed our way.

"Go fetch more water," Amos scowled, when I ran to tell him. His jaw muscles twitched as he clenched and unclenched his teeth. "These folks gonna be mighty thirsty. With a bit a luck, they'll water up then keep on goin' instead 'a hangin' 'round here till mornin'."

Slowly, the long trail of wagons snaked its way down the hill. Bony oxen and tired ponies leaned into their heavy loads, flanks heaving. Several dogs trudged alongside the wagons, tongues lolling from the heat.

"Howdy folks!" a tall, slender man greeted us, a sheen of perspiration covering his face. Beside him sat a tired-looking woman, rocking a whimpering baby.

Amos nodded curtly, a strained smile on his lips. "Name's Amos Perkins. I'm the manager here. Where ya all headed?"

"Oregon," the man replied, wiping the back of his neck with a kerchief.

Amos nodded. "Can I git you folks anythin' on yer way through?"

It was hard to miss the hint behind Amos' words. I moved away, embarrassed by his uncaring attitude.

The man climbed down, swiping an arm across his forehead. "Thank you, Mr. Perkins. Name's John Clarkson. I'm the wagon master. We sure could use a break till it's a bit cooler. Maybe git a drink of water?"

"Billy here will git ya all a drink, then you can take your cattle down to the springs," Amos said.

Mr. Clarkson lifted one arm, signaling to the wagons lined up behind him. Within minutes, our quiet little station was overcome with a noisy mayhem of crying, yelling, neighing, squalling, bellowing, and barking. As I poured two bucketfuls of water into the rain barrels, I suddenly found myself surrounded by a crowd of kids eagerly reaching for the dipper.

"Can I have a drink, mister?" a little girl asked, gazing up at me with bright amber eyes that matched her hair. Her pink dressed was rumpled and frayed at the hem. Her feet were bare.

"Of course," I said, smiling.

Filling the dipper, I handed it to her. She brushed back a tangle of reddish-brown hair with work-roughened hands, then took the dipper from me. I doubted she was older than five years of age yet she looked so much older.

While most kids laughed and played after school, this little girl probably helped with chores until her mother tucked her in at night, in the back of the cramped wagon, between a hope chest and the family's dishes.

Behind her, another little girl caught my attention. She had the prettiest face with gorgeous blue eyes. Her yellow dress, patched at the elbows, hung loosely on her small frame. She was also barefoot.

I offered her a friendly smile. Instead of returning the smile, she hid behind her mother's skirt.

"It's okay, Caroline," her mother said, urging her forward. "Take a drink."

Caroline's mother stepped forward. Her long black hair had escaped the ribbon at the back of her neck, several strands hanging loosely about her face.

"Thank you," she said, taking the dipper. Her voice so soft I could barely hear her over the clamor. Instead of guzzling the water like the others, she sipped slowly, savoring every drop. Gradually, the tight lines in her weather-worn face relaxed a little bit.

Handing the dipper back, she offered me a thin smile, then turned and shuffled back to her wagon. Her shoulders drooped as though she carried a heavy load. I felt so sorry for these people. Like me, they were looking for a better life. No matter what came their way, they kept moving, each day the same as the one before, never giving up, chasing a dream always just out of their reach.

"Hey, Paul!" a gruff voice bellowed over the clamor of voices. "Gimme a hand with this wheel!"

My head whipped up at the sound of the gravelly voice. I'd recognize it anywhere. Every muscle in my body instantly tensed. My eyes skimmed through the crowd, my gaze landing on a man with thin eyebrows, a sharp nose, and a birthmark along his chin. His face had struck me the first time I'd seen him. I'd thought he looked like a hawk. I couldn't remember where I'd seen him but knew he spelled trouble.

Shoving the dipper into the hands of the next person in line, I picked up two empty buckets, then skulked off towards the barn, head lowered. I wasn't sure who he was but knew I needed to avoid him at all costs.

I wasn't quick enough. The man saw me and yelled out. "Hey, kid, how 'bout a drink of water?"

My heart thudded in my chest, faster and louder, as I remembered watching this man argue with Pa just a few months ago over some money he had loaned Pa.

I began to run. If I could reach the barn, I might be able to hide in one of the stalls until everyone left. I dodged behind one of the wagons, and pressed against it, panting and shivering with fear.

"Hey kid," the man hollered. I shrank back against the wagon but it was too late.

He'd seen me.

I was trapped.

Chapter Fourteen

"Hey, boy," the man said, bearing down on me. "Didn't ya hear me? I could use a drink."

I lowered my head. I couldn't let him see my face just in case he recognized me. This man could ruin everything. If only he would step back so I could pass. Instead, he grabbed my shoulder with bruising force and spun me around. He reeked of tobacco mingled with sweat.

"I said...," he began, then stopped mid-sentence. His cold, penetrating gaze searched my face "Say, don't I know you?"

My heart lurched. I was in deep trouble. I swallowed hard then shook my head, my voice too shaky to speak.

The man tightened his grip on my shoulder. I winced as his fingers pressed into my flesh. The bucket slipped from my hands, landing on the ground with a *clank*.

"I'm sure I've seen ya before," he said, squatting to get a better look at my face.

"No, s..., sir," I stammered. Pain shot through my shoulder and down my arm.

"Hey, ain't you Ray's boy?"

My legs were shaking so much they nearly buckled under me.

"No, sir. I'm... I'm an orphan."

"I think yer lyin' to me." His gaze bore into mine. "I'm 'most positive yer Ray's son."

He snapped his fingers as though trying to match name and face.

"Can't 'member yer name jus' now, but I do know Ray's been lookin' for you. Says you knocked 'im out cold, then ran off with all his money."

His words were like a punch to the stomach. I couldn't breathe, couldn't think, couldn't move. Of all the boldfaced, hurtful lies!

"I didn't...," I began, anger spewing from my mouth. I stopped short as I realized the worst I could do was to respond to the lie.

"No... sir," I stuttered. "I told ya. I don't have no pa. I'm an orphan."

"Are ya, now?" His jaw hardened. "'cause ya look jus' like Ray's son. Wonder if yer pa would offer me money if I turned ya in?"

His hand on my shoulder grew stronger as I tried to break loose from his grasp. I let out a gasp of pain.

"All right, folks, let's move down to the springs." Mr. Jackson's voice carried over the ruckus. "Men, to your wagons."

I felt the man's grip ease. With one last, hard look, he released me. "Count yerself lucky, boy. If I was headin' the other way, I'd 'a taken ya back to yer pa. Asked for a reward."

Turning away, he sauntered back to his wagon. I was so shaken, I dropped onto the nearby chopping block, watching as the wagon train headed down to the springs. Wagons creaked as weary oxen and ponies lumbered down the dirt path, kicking up clouds of dust.

As the last wagon pulled out, Caroline's little face poked out the back of the swooping canvas covering. She waved at me then smiled. I waved back then winced at the pain in my shoulder where the brute had squeezed it so hard.

"Sakes alive! The man almost let the cat outta the bag," I mumbled in a low voice. I'd thought I would be safe way out here but it wasn't true. I wasn't safe anywhere.

From behind me came a rustling sound. I whirled around to find Amos leaning casually against the barn wall, staring at me. He had a strange look in his eyes.

Just, *how much had he overheard? And, what would he do about it?*

Chapter Fifteen

Darkness had descended on the valley by the time I headed for bed. I was eager to put this day behind me. A jumble of emotions bubbled within me; fear, hurt, disappointment, betrayal, and a deep, unexplainable sadness which hurt more than any physical pain.

For a while, I paused, listening to the soft night sounds. At times, this world seemed so immense, especially at night as I stood under the canopy of stars flickering in the vast, seamless sky. Today, the world seemed far too small. Here I was, in the middle of nowhere, yet I'd still run into someone who knew my pa. For such a small world as mine, it sure was big on bullies.

"Speaking of bullies," I asked the crescent moon, "how much did Amos hear?"

It was possible he'd heard every word. If so, would he tell Mr. Slade or hold it over me like some threat?

Somewhere in the distance, wolves howled, their woeful cries reflecting my own mood. *A-woooo. A-woooo.* Their howls no longer frightened me. I had grown used to it, just like Mr. Hammond said. Their nightly chorus was part of this land, as natural as the chirping of crickets, or the quacking of wild geese as they flew overhead.

Rubbing my sore shoulder, I opened the barn door then slipped inside, ready to grab my blanket so I could head down to the springs to sleep in the shelter of the willow tree. All I could think about - all I wanted to think about – was sleep.

As I closed the door behind me, I sensed something wasn't right. Something had stirred up the horses. They were edgy, snorting as they banged against the sides of their stalls.

Wary, I lifted my lantern and glanced around. Nothing seemed to be out of place. Slowly, I crept forward, pausing briefly to glance in each stall. I couldn't see anything unusual, yet something had spooked them.

A strange scuffling noise stopped me mid-stride. I froze, straining to listen. Something or someone, was lurking in the shadows. An opossum? A bobcat? An outlaw?

I stood frozen, unable to move, unsure what to do. If I fetched Amos and it ended up being some small animal just looking for a dark place to sleep, I would be making a fool of myself. I'd done plenty of that since I'd arrived.

I decided to check it out on my own first. I tried to silence the pounding of my heart as I listened in the darkness. There it was again! It sounded like nails scratching against something. The sound seemed to be coming from the tack room.

I looked about for some sort of weapon. My gaze fell on a long, skinny object leaning against the back wall; the pitchfork. Holding it in front of me, its sharp tines pointed forward, I inched across the barn, squinting through the gloom at the dark corners of the tack room. My blood ran cold as I spotted a dark shape, about the size of a human being, huddled beneath Amos' workbench.

Terrified, I spun around, running as fast as my legs would carry me, dropping the pitchfork in my haste. Sprinting across the yard to the soddy, I flung open the door.

"Amos... come... quick."

Amos was perched on the edge of his bunk, bare chested, his suspenders hanging loosely about his waist.

"What now?" He yawned loudly as he pulled off his boot.

"The... there's somethin'... in... the barn," I stuttered, pointing a trembling finger towards the door.

"Prob'ly jus' some ol' coon lookin' fer a few scraps," Amos grumbled. "Jus' leave it be till mornin'."

"It can't be," I insisted, shuffling from one foot to the other. "I saw it... it's this big." I spread my arms wide. "Ya gotta come!"

"Okay, okay," Amos snapped, stuffing his large feet back into his boots. "Don't git huffy."

Shoving one suspender over a bare shoulder, Amos grabbed his rifle, flung the door open, and marched across the yard, mumbling under his breath. I followed, fearful yet curious. What if it was an outlaw or a large wolf?

Mr. Hammond had said the wolves out here had fangs big as arrowheads. If it was wounded, Amos might have an advantage. But he would still have only one shot before the animal or person would be upon him, biting, clawing, and tearing at his flesh.

Standing just inside the doorway, Amos paused to listen. Other than the horses fidgeting in their stalls, nothing stirred. Grabbing the lantern from my shaky hand, Amos held it up then swept it left and right.

"Where?"

I pointed towards the tack room. "In... in there."

Amos moved into the tack room, raking the darkness with his lantern. The feeble light cast odd shadows on the walls and ceilings. I shivered, imagining one of those shadows jumping out at me.

"Don't see nothin'."

I peered cautiously around Amos.

"There!" I said, pointing to the bulky shadow under the workbench.

Amos snorted. "That's jus' a pile of ol' harnesses." He yanked an old cloth off a stack of broken hitches. "Now if ya don't mind, I'm gonna git me some sleep."

I hung my head as Amos headed for the door, grumbling something about fools under his breath. I was furious at myself.

"Blast it, ya little twit," Amos yelled, as he stepped on the tines of the pitchfork I'd left on the floor in my rush to get help. The handle popped up and hit him in the face.

"One of these days, yer gonna be the death of me…." Amos yelled, jabbing the pitchfork into a nearby pile of straw.

Amos stopped mid-sentence as a loud, throaty growl resonated through the barn. Amos turned to look at me, surprised. Grabbing the pitchfork, he placed a finger over his lips to shush me.

I think it's a bit late for that, I thought, but kept the comment to myself.

Chapter Sixteen

Amos handed me the pitchfork. "You move the straw aside, I'll shoot," he whispered.

Raising his rifle, Amos rested the stock against his right shoulder.

"Ready?"

"Ready," I whispered.

"Now!"

I planted my feet, ready to bolt, then scooped up a layer of hay. A pair of glassy brown eyes peered out at us, like two little orbs floating in the night sky. Its fur stood up along its back and a menacing growl rose from its throat. Whatever it was, it was not human.

Slowly the creature rose to its feet. I stepped back a pace, terrified it would leap out at us.

I laughed as I suddenly figured out what it was. "It's just a dog!"

The dirty, scraggy dog bared its teeth, snarling as it cowered beneath the hay.

"The beast must 'a come with the wagon train," Amos grumbled, his finger closing on the trigger.

"Don't kill 'im," I yelled, as I realized Amos meant to shoot the dog.

Amos' finger tightened on the trigger.

"Stop!" I yelled, jumping between the dog and the gun.

"Stupid fool!" Amos hollered, lowering his rifle. "Never step in front of a loaded gun! I could 'a shot you!"

Glaring at the dog, Amos shoved me aside, then raised his weapon again.

"Don't!" I screamed, grabbing Amos' sleeve.

Bang!

The sound exploded through the barn, terrifyingly loud. The horses cried out and banged against the walls of their stalls. Covering my face, I whimpered. I was too scared to look at the dog.

Was he dead? "You meddlin' child!" Amos hollered. "Look what ya done."

Spreading my fingers, I peeked. Amos wasn't staring at the dog, nor was he even looking at me. Instead, he was looking straight up. I followed his gaze to a bullet-shaped hole in the roof.

"Well, ya don't jus' shoot a dog 'cause it's sleepin' in yer barn," I shouted. "It's prob'ly jus' hungry or scared."

"Listen up, boy," Amos snarled. "You could have gotten someone killed with yer foolish antics. Now I have a hole in the roof that you are going to fix."

I lowered my head. "I'm really sorry 'bout the roof. But please don't shoot the dog."

"Can't ya see this bag 'a bones sick? Be a mercy to took 'im outta his misery."

"Please, Amos." I gave him a pleading look. "At least give 'im a chance. I… I can fix 'im up."

"He ain't worth it," Amos growled.

"Please."

Amos rubbed his neck, thinking. "Ya got one day," he finally said. "If this flea-bag ain't up and about by this time tomorrow, then I'll have to shoot 'it."

Tucking his rifle under one arm, Amos marched out the door. "It better not mess with the horses either," he yelled over his shoulder, slamming the door behind him with enough force to rattle the whole barn.

I squatted to take a better look at the mangy dog. Ears back, the dog growled, his teeth bared in a snarl. His fur stood straight up, its back arched in warning.

"It's okay," I crooned, using the same soft, soothing voice that worked with the horses. "I ain't gonna hurt ya none."

The dog's growls subsided to a half-hearted grumble. He was a medium-size male, underweight, and dirty as a pig in a sty.

"You thirsty?"

The dog looked at me with sad eyes.

"Stay here while I fetch some water."

Slowly, I rose to my feet then backed away, eyes locked on the dog the whole time. I didn't want any surprises. Once clear of the stall, I turned and ran to the rain barrel where I filled a bucket with water then carried it back to the dog. The poor creature still laid where I'd left him.

I placed the bucket on the floor beside him. "This is for you."

The dog eyed me warily, uncertain if he could trust me.

"Come on," I urged. "It's just water."

The dog stood on wobbly legs, ears lowered, tail tucked between his legs. He sniffed the bucket, lapped up the water as though he hadn't drunk in days, then laid down again.

Slow as a snail, I reached out, my palm up, ready to yank my hand away should he try to bite me. The dog stretched out his neck, sniffed my hand, then whimpered softly. Resting his head on his front paws, he let a sigh.

"Where did you come from?" I said, watching him rest. "Did you belong to some little boy or girl from the wagon train?" I hoped not, because they would be missing him tonight.

Then I thought about the man who'd grabbed my arm. "One thing's for sure. If you were with that nasty man, you're much better off with me."

I dropped down beside him. He didn't seem to mind. "So, my name's Billy. I'm sure ya have a name too but seein as ya can't tell me, I'll have to call ya Mutt until I find a better name."

The dog looked at me, his eyes sad and heavy.

"I sure hope ya git better, 'cause I don't want that ol' coot to shoot ya. He's a mean one and he won't think twice about getting' rid of you if ya don't get up and walk."

With a whimper, the dog closed his eyes, as though it was all just too much for him. Within seconds he was asleep.

I laid down beside him, watching as the dog snoozed. He seemed so harmless with his soft little ears and the tip of his little pink tongue poking out between his lips. Flipping onto my back, I closed my eyes.

Don't get attached to the dog, I told myself. *Amos might change his mind and decide to shoot him come morning.*

Deep down, I knew I was kidding myself. It was too late. This dog had already wormed its way into my heart.

Chapter Seventeen

A scratching sound yanked me from a deep sleep. *Scratch... scratch.*

I struggled to open my eyes.

Scratch.... Scratch.

Then I remembered the dog. I quickly rose and hurried toward the noise. It was the dog, standing at the door, pawing to get out.

"Yer up!" I squealed.

The dog glanced up at me and wagged his tail.

"Well, that's a good sign," I chuckled, opening the door for him.

The dog twitched his nose in the warm morning breeze then limped out into the yard to relieve himself. He was having a hard time walking, but at least he was trying. Limping slowly back into the barn, he dropped on the ground and started licking his paws.

"Look at her paws! They're so red and sore. No wonder ya don't wanna walk."

The dog gazed up at me, his droopy brown eyes twin pools of misery.

I reached out to stroke him. "Ya poor thing."

The dog responded with a thump of his tail.

"Lemme git ya some more water. After breakfast, I'll sneak ya a few scraps."

The dog thumped his tail once more, then rolled onto his side and dozed off.

I refilled the dog's water dish, headed to the soddy. Amos was already up, broody and silent as he sipped his coffee. I was glad he wasn't in a chatty mood because I didn't want to talk about the dog or the man who'd threatened me yesterday.

All these thoughts ran through my mind as I cooked bacon and heated up some leftover cornbread. Amos grunted as I set the hot food on the table, then set into it like a ravenous wolf.

As soon as he'd finished, Amos pushed back his seat. Reaching above the door, he took down the gun then walked out. My stomach felt like it was being squeezed in a vice.

"No!" I screamed, running after him. "Don't, please don't!"

Big, heart-wrenching sobs shook my body. "Please don't kill him."

Amos turned, staring at me wide-eyed.

"Please don't," I begged, grabbing his arm.

"Whatcha jawing about?" Amos said, shaking off my hand.

"Please don't kill the dog. Please give 'im a chance. You said you wouldn't if he was up by today but he did. He did. He walked out of the barn to pee, then walked back in. He's restin' now but I swear, he did walk."

"I ain't fixin' to shoot the dog, jus' thought I'd go catch us a rabbit for dinner."

Weak-kneed, I sank to the ground and cried. This time, the tears were tears of relief. For now, at least, the dog was safe.

"Git yerself together, boy," Amos growled, shaking his head as he disappeared around the back of the house.

I sniffed, wiped my nose on my sleeve, then stood and lurched back into the house. I put some leftovers on a plate, then hustled back to the barn. The dog was still in the same spot, paws twitching as he slept.

Dropping down beside him, I held out a strip of bacon. The dog's eyes snapped open. He pushed himself up and snatched the meat out of my fingers.

"Hey, ya didn't even chew that up," I laughed, holding out another piece, then another. "Jus' don't tell Amos I fed you, our food."

While the dog finished eating the bacon and cornbread, I ran a hand over his fur. It was grimey with dried mud and burs. He needed a bath. Though noticeably underweight, I doubted I could lift him, let alone lug him down to the springs.

When I tried to check his paws, the dog let out a yelp. "Sorry. Didn't mean to hurt ya."

I filled a bucket with water, then grabbed an old sack from the tack room and knelt on the floor. I dipped the sack into the water, then gently rubbed it across the dog's mottled coat. Filthy water dribbled onto the floor.

"Ya sure don't take a bath very often, do ya?"

The dog gazed up at me with soft brown eyes and thumped his tail.

"That's okay, neither does Amos." I giggled. The dog reacted with another thump of his tail.

Once I'd washed the mud off, I ran a curry comb through his fur. "Ya sure do look a lot better," I said, stroking his dark, shiny coat.

Thump, thump, thump, went the dog's tail.

"We gotta do somethin' 'bout yer paws, though," I said, gently holding one of his front paws to check the pads. They were red and raw. The dog flinched and whimpered softly but didn't pull away. Ever so lightly, I began dabbing at the sores with the wet rag, trying to dislodge some of the dirt that had caked in the cracks.

"Ya might wanna rub some of this into his paws."

I jumped. I hadn't heard Amos come in.

"This is what I use on the horses," he mumbled, handing me a jar of ointment.

How long has he been standing behind me? I wondered, taking the jar.

"Jus' make sure yer regular chores git done," Amos said over his shoulder, then stomped out of the barn.

I stared at the man's back, mouth hanging wide open with shock. "Well, I'll be," I whispered. "Guess he can be nice if he has a mind to."

I opened the jar, dipped my finger into the greasy ointment, then rubbed it into the dog's pads, working it gently into the cracks. "That should feel better."

Thump, thump, thump.

I let out a heartfelt laugh. "Yer welcome. Now I best git to work, 'fore Amos changes his mind 'bout keepin' ya."

Throughout the day, I checked on the dog, rubbing a little more ointment into his paws at each visit. Most of the time he slept, rising only to go out to relieve himself. As evening came on, I was thrilled to see he wasn't limping as much.

That night, I slept with the dog. As I settled in the hay beside him, the dog scooted closer. Then he laid his head on my chest. Tears began to trickle down my cheeks. For the very first time, someone wanted me. For the first time, someone was showing me some love.

"Love ya, too," I whispered, running a hand over his soft ears.

I could feel the steady rhythm of the dog's heartbeat, the warmth of his body. It made my heart tingle with happiness.

Dapples of moonlight streamed down on us through the bullet-sized hole in the roof. I laughed.

"You know something?"

The dog perked his ears.

"Yer one lucky dog. Sure, am glad Amos gave ya a second chance."

Chance; it was such a fitting name.

"You like the name 'Chance'?"

Thump, thump, thump.

Wrapping an arm around him, I snuggled closer. "Ya know something, Chance? Yer the best friend ever."

Chance licked my face, his pink tongue wet and rough on my cheek. It was a strange feeling, but in a good way. It was Chance's way of telling me he loved me. I smiled as the dog fell asleep, his body curled up against mine, his head on my chest.

I broke into a huge grin. For the first time in years, I fell asleep with a smile on my face and joy in my heart.

At last, I had a friend.

Chapter Eighteen

My life changed after Chance arrived. It felt as though I'd begun a new chapter in my life. I slept better, smiled more, even caught myself singing as I worked. The loneliness was gone.

For the first time, I was able to love and be loved in return. Not the complicated, awkward human kind of love, but a comfortable, easy friendship. Even Amos' grumpiness didn't irk me as much as it once did.

For the first few days, Chance followed me around as I did my chores. He was loyal, unselfish, smart, fun, and brought joy to each day – basically, everything Amos was not.

All day long, he frisked around my legs, ears flapping as he darted this way and that. He was a great listener, tilting his head to one side as I talked. With his ears pricked and his sappy brown eyes staring right at me, I could almost believe he understood every word I said.

Chance's paws healed quickly. He also lost his sickly appearance. He grew stronger and, within a couple of days, he was romping around. Nose to the ground, he sniffed out new scents and chased birds, squirrels, possums, basically anything that moved.

Some days, while I was busy cooking or cleaning out the horses' stalls, Chance would run off then return with some gift, dropping it at my feet like a token of gratitude. Some of his gifts were not so nice, like chewed-up frogs or some animal carcass which had been baking in the hot sun for several days. Others were useful, like freshly killed jackrabbits or prairie chickens which I'd skin, then cook into a stew.

Chance loved the horses. I would often find him sitting just inside the corral fence, watching as they galloped round and round. They'd quickly adjusted to the dog's presence and didn't seem to mind him hanging around.

When the mood struck him, Chance joined in the fun, running alongside as the horses cantered around the enclosure, keeping just enough distance between him and the horses so he wouldn't get trampled.

Amos, on the other hand, remained aloof towards the dog. He wasn't mean to Chance or cruel by any means. He simply ignored Chance as if he were a nuisance which was basically how he treated me. Amos also insisted the dog stay outside and wouldn't let him come into the house.

"Git outta my way, ya worthless flea-bag," Amos would grumble whenever Chance ran up to him, tongue lolling. Yet Amos never laid a hand – or foot – on the dog. For this, I was grateful.

Eventually, the hot dry summer days gave way to a crisp fall. The leaves on the cottonwoods traded their summer green color for autumn-gold. After my day's work was done, I'd bring Chance down to the pools where I swam while he chased rabbits into their burrows. He loved to shove his nose into their narrow tunnels, kicking up moist dirt with his front paws as he tried to dig his way in after them.

One brown fox squirrel liked to taunt Chance, scolding him with a strident kuk-kuk-kuk from the branch of the old, hollow, oak tree where he lived. Chance would bark, scrabbling wildly at the tree trunk until I finally called him off or the squirrel grew tired of the game and disappeared through the hole in the trunk.

Afterwards, we'd curl up together under the willow's silvery-green dome. As fall stretched on, the autumn sun muted the willow's leaves to a soft harvest yellow. Days grew shorter, nights longer.

Chilly days turned into cold, nippy nights. Chance and I eventually had to give up our golden fortress to sleep in the warmth of the barn. I was thankful to be able to snuggle against Chance's warm body each night.

I no longer swam in the springs; the water was too cold. Chance didn't seem to mind so I'd take him down to the water's edge each evening and watch him splash in the pools.

Propped against a cottonwood, I waited for the first star to appear in the blue-black sky so I could make a wish. It was always the same one; someday I would be a Pony Express rider.

With winter fast approaching, I decided to sort through the food supplies. Some of them had gone bad and had to be thrown out. Some supplies had been used up, so I wrote a list of foods we needed to keep on hand in case bad weather stopped Mr. Hammond from coming. We had lots of cases of beans, but beans aren't the best when you have to share a small space because you're snowed in.

One frosty morning, I decided to clean up the mess under the bottom bunk. I swept away the cobwebs, then hauled boxes out from under the bed. Much of the clutter was just dusty odds and ends or old harnesses chewed useless by mice.

One box, stuffed far into a dark corner, was tied with several strands of string. Curious, I pulled it out then dusted it off. It was no bigger than a cigar box. Although I had a feeling I might be snooping, I wanted to see what was in the box. I rose to check where Amos was and was happy to see he was on the other side of the yard, repairing one of the fence posts. It seemed like he would be busy for a while. Relieved, I sat back down on the floor and picked up the box. Placing it in my lap, I loosened the knot, pulled off the string, then lifted the lid.

Inside was a stack of photos. The first photo was of a woman sitting in a chair, alone. She was beautiful, with long auburn hair spilling out from under her sun bonnet. Her hair flowed over her shoulders, down the front of her lacy dress. She couldn't have been more than seventeen or eighteen when this photo was taken. She seemed to be laughing at something or someone, a bright smile lighting up her beautiful face.

The next photo was a family portrait. A severe-looking man frowned at the camera. Beside him was a young woman I guessed to be his wife. On her lap sat a small boy. To her left, stood an older boy, probably about ten years old.

On her right stood a pretty, youthful girl who appeared to be about eleven or twelve. I immediately recognized the striking face from the first photo, even though she was several years younger in this picture.

Who were these people? I wondered. *Why does Amos keep their photos closed in a box, sealed with string, and hidden under his bed? Could this stunning woman be a girl he'd once loved?*

I chuckled at the thought. Somehow, I just couldn't imagine grumpy old Amos falling in love with anyone. Then again, maybe she'd broken his heart which could explain why he was always so grumpy.

"What in tarnation are ya doin'?"

I jumped. The photos slipped from my hands, dropping to the ground.

Amos' large figure filled the doorway. I'd been so wrapped up in the photos I hadn't heard him come in.

Amos' gaze fell on the photos laying on the floor. His face turned red with rage.

"Git... out!" he screamed, pointing to the door.

Scrambling to my feet, I ran past Amos, dashed out of the house, then took off running across the yard. Breathless, I dropped to the ground behind the barn, shaking with fear. Chance rushed after me and huddled against me.

Several minutes later, Amos came to find me. His eyes were bright with fury. "Ya had no business touchin' my stuff, ya hear me? Those pictures are none of yer business."

I nodded. To my horror, a single sob escaped my lips. Amos slammed his hand against the barn wall, startling Chance and me. Amos thundered off, his boots pounding the hard-packed dirt. Within seconds, I heard the *whoosh, slam, whoosh, slam* of the ax as Amos chopped away at the log pile.

Pulling Chance into my arms, I hugged him tight. The dog whimpered.

"The man's a mean ol' cuss," I sniveled.

Chance didn't say a word, but he didn't have to. His presence was comfort enough.

Chapter Nineteen

Several days passed in silence. Amos and I went about our chores, arranging our daily tasks around the others to avoid seeing each other. Amos was more than just angry, he was hostile.

Then one crisp autumn night, I was startled out of a deep sleep. I slowly became aware that Chance was growling. The deep-throated, menacing rumble rising from his chest made my skin crawl. In their stalls, the horses were also restless, whinnying and stomping their feet.

For a minute I laid quietly, listening. I came fully awake at the sound of hushed voices.

"Shhh!" a deep voice whispered. "Now ya woke the stupid dog with all yer stomping."

"I ain't stomping," another voice answered. "I can't help it if I can't see where I'm goin'. It's dark as blazes out here."

Crash!

A tin bucket rattled as it tumbled across the yard.

Someone cursed. The sound sent a trickle of fear up my spine.

Chance flew to the door and threw his body against it, growling and barking like some ferocious beast. For a split second, I thought about burying deeper in the straw. Then I thought about doing the opposite and calling out to warn whoever was prowling outside that we had guns. Whatever their reason for being here, it certainly wasn't a friendly one.

"What's barking?" a gruff voice said.

"A dog, you idiot!" a deeper voice snapped.

"Mud Springs station don't have no dog," the first man insisted.

"Well, apparently they do now, ya fool! You shoot the mutt while I gather the horses."

Instantly, my fear vanished, replaced by hot rage. No one was going to come near my dog! Cautiously, I inched my way to the door. Wrapping an arm around his neck, I pulled Chance away from the door, dragging him into a dark corner. Grabbing the pitchfork, I gripped it in one hand while holding fast to Chance with the other. Chance pulled frantically on my hand, struggling to free himself.

"Stop pullin'," I said, tightening my grip as Chance barked and clawed the dirt floor. "

From the dark corner where I crouched, ready to pounce, I watched the barn door open a crack. I couldn't see anyone in the gloom. The door opened wider. A dark shape stepped over the threshold, looming in the doorway, large and frightening against the blackness of night. I couldn't see his face but caught the gleam of metal. He was holding a revolver. Stifling the scream that threatened to break loose, I firmed my grip on Chance.

The man lit a lantern, lighting up his face. I slapped a hand over my mouth to stifle a shriek of terror. Most of the man's nose was missing. His cheeks were scarred from burns. The sneer on his lips brought the word evil to mind. I was alone with a crazed dog and a cold-hearted killer.

Behind this evil person stood another man, tall, lean, his long hair greased into a ponytail.

Chance could no longer stand it. Squeezing out of my arms, he shot across the barn.

"Kill 'im, Tom" the first man yelled, handing him the revolver.

Weak with horror, I watched as Tom lifted the gun and aimed it at Chance. But Chance was quicker. Snarling like a rabid wolf, Chance vaulted into the air, landing on Ponytail's chest, taking him to the ground.

"Aaargh!" the prowler screamed, dropping the gun as Chance sank his teeth into the man's wrist.

I lunged forward, pitchfork raised above my head, then slammed the hard metal tines down on the guy's skull. All those hours of mucking stables and hauling water had built up my strength; the man gave a loud grunt then went limp, falling to the ground, his gun beside him.

The other crook dove for the revolver, but Chance was standing over it, feet planted, teeth bared threateningly.

"Stupid mutt," the intruder snarled as he lobbed a kick towards Chance.

I raised the pitchfork, ready to hit the man when the crack of a gunshot rang thought the air. A bullet plowed into the ground at the man's feet. He froze mid-step, his hand inches from the gun still laying on the floor.

"Don't... even... think... about it," a deep voice growled.

Amos' large form filled the doorway. His face was dark with rage.

"Back away from the gun," Amos ordered.

The man straightened ever so slowly, his lips curling into a sneer. "You really gonna shoot me, Amos?"

"Hello Dan," Amos said. "You think ya can just walk in here and grab a few horses? Over my dead body!" he snarled, stepping over to the revolver. With one hard kick, he sent it skimming across the floor.

In that one second of distraction, Dan rushed forward. With a rapid swing of his foot, he kicked the rifle out of Amos' hand, then rammed Amos in the stomach with a fierce punch of his elbow.

Amos staggered backwards, his eyes wide with surprise. Before he could recover, Dan slammed his fist into Amos' face. A sickening *crack* rang through the air as it smashed Amos's nose. Amos doubled over, blood streaming down his face.

I stepped towards the rustler, pitchfork in hand. He looked at me with a sneer.

"Beggin' fer some too, are ya?" Dan mocked as he knocked the pitchfork out of my hands then slammed it down on my head. I fell into a heap, dizzy with pain.

"Leave the boy out of this," Amos said, trying to stand up.

With one quick movement, the rustler struck a sharp blow to the back of Amos' neck. Amos sucked in a deep breath then stumbled backwards. Horrified, I watched Amos fall to his knees, then collapse.

In one swift move, Chance left the gun and lunged at Dan. His strong jaws locked around the man's leg. Dan let out a howl of pain.

"Git off me, ya stupid mutt," Dan yelled, shaking his leg to loosen the dog's powerful jaws.

Chance held firm, clinging with all his might to Dan's shin. The man swung his leg, slamming Chance against the wall with a ghastly *thud*. A loud yelp, then Chance crumpled in a heap.

"Chance!" I screamed, crawling to his side.

I pulled the dog against my chest. He didn't move.

"No! No!" I sobbed, burying my face in Chance's soft fur, my body shaking with sobs.

The rustler's focus turned to me. His evil smile showed a row of tobacco-stained teeth. "What about you, little boy? You gonna fight or run like a coward?"

Legs shaky as a lamb's, I scrambled to my feet.

"You beast," I hissed.

The scoundrel had possibly killed Amos and Chance. I had little to lose.

The man took a step forward. "What? Don't like the way I play?"

He took another step closer. I stumbled backwards. Step-by-step, he continued to advance, driving me back until I smacked against a wall.

He'd backed me into a corner.

The game was over.

There was no escape.

"Whatcha gonna do now, tough-guy?" His mocking face was so close I could smell whiskey on his breath.

"Yer nothin' but a beast," I screamed, then spat in his face.

His laugh was cruel, evil, edged with hatred. Taking another step forward, he aimed a punch at me. I'd had plenty of practice dodging Pa's fist, so I ducked just in time. Dan's fist slammed into the wall.

With a scream of pain, Dan grabbed me with the other hand, holding me by the collar as he lifted me off my feet. Like a hooked fish, I twisted and thrashed, wrestling to free myself. The more I struggled, the more he tightened his grip.

"Lemme go," I yelled, kicking him in the shins. "Lemme go."

"As you wish," the man said, then he flung me against the wall.

Slithering down the wall, I struck the ground with a *thump*. It felt as though all the air had been sucked out from my lungs. With a loud gasp, I pulled in enough breath to rise to my knees.

All the fury and hatred within me boiled to the surface; I was overcome with a strength I never knew I had. With a strangled cry, I threw all my weight against Dan's legs, knocking him backwards.

Caught off guard, Dan staggered back. But he was off-balance. Arms flailing, he toppled to the ground, his head striking the lantern.

Crash!

The lantern hit the ground, shattering the glass dome. Instantly, bright orange flames leapt into the air as they lit the hay on fire.

The barn was on fire!

Chapter Twenty

For a second or two, I was too stunned to move, watching as bright flames licked the barn floor. When I opened my mouth to scream all that came out was a gurgle.

"Tom!" In one swift movement, Dan jumped to his feet and rushed over to Tom. Tom!"

Tom blinked then slowly opened his eyes. At the sight of the flames, he staggered to his feet. Leaning on his partner, the pair stumbled out into the dark night.

Rushing to Amos' side, I fell to my knees. Amos lay against the wall like a rag doll.

"Amos," I screamed, shaking him. "Amos… wake up! The barn is on fire!"

No response.

"Amos! Amos!"

Amos finally moved, struggling to open his eyes between his puffy eyelids. His face had already started to swell. His shirt was drenched in blood.

"Up!" I yelled again. "Git up, Amos!"

Amos struggled to get his legs under him then grabbed his stomach, crying out in pain. Rolling onto his hands and knees, he pushed up on to his feet. He was too weak, too wobbly. He sagged against the wall.

"Don't worry 'bout me. Just see to the horses," Amos croaked, swaying dangerously.

I took off at a run. Thankfully, we had a small number of horses boarding with us that night. The Pony Express horses were worth the most, so they were my first concern. I immediately headed for Thunder's stall. What I found was a crazed beast. The horse's eyes were wide with fear as he stomped and shook his head.

I seized the latch to unlock the gate, but the metal wouldn't slide free. It was jammed.

"Come on, come on," I fumed, yanking and pulling in turn. But the latch wouldn't move.

"If only I had my knife," I grumbled.

Frantically, I searched for some sort of blade.

"Confound it!" I yelled, kicking the gate in frustration.

On the other side, Thunder kicked back.

"That's it!" Grabbing one of the shovels nearby, I raised it above my head, then smacked it down on Thunder's rump. With a loud scream, the mustang kicked out, his hooves striking the half door, shattering it to pieces. I ducked just in time to avoid the shards of wood flying left and right.

Rushing in, I untied the halter from the tie ring then covered his eyes with a feed sack so he wouldn't panic if he saw the flames.

"Good boy," I crooned, struggling to calm the frantic animal. "I'll git ya outta here."

I guided him out the back door and released him into the corral.

A scream erupted from inside. Dropping Thunder's halter, I raced back inside to find Amos doubled over, his face twisted with pain. He was clutching his right hand. Beads of sweat trickled down his face as he shoved his burnt hand into a bucket of water then sucked in a sharp breath.

The sickening smell of burned skin made my stomach queasy. Flames flickered where the lamp had fallen, although most of the fire hadn't moved beyond to the common area and tack room. Grabbing a bucket of water, I flung it on the fire, the flames hissing like a frightened cat.

In their stalls, the other horses were stomping and snorting with fright.

"Git them out," Amos choked.

My eyes smarted from the smoke. I blinked rapidly to clear them.

"Go!" Amos barked.

Dropping the bucket, I ran back to the stalls. One by one, I led the rest of the horses out to the corral, then closed the back door to keep them from wandering back in. The horses were safe, I could focus on helping Amos. He was stubbornly fighting the fire despite his burned hand.

I dashed back and forth from the barn to the rain barrels, refilling the buckets with water while Amos doused the last lingering flames. Grabbing some feed bags, I plunged them into the nearest bucket then laid the wet bags on the flames, smothering the last of the fire till nothing was left but a pile of wet ashes. A few harmless threads of smoke rose into the air.

The fire had damaged a couple of inside walls along with part of the tack room. Considering what could have happened, I was thankful the barn hadn't suffered more damage. With all the wood and hay in the building, we could have lost everything.

"We did it, Amos!" I yelled, turning to look at Amos.

The man was a sorry sight. Sweat and blood, mingled together, trickled down his sooty face. His nose was twice its usual size. Tiny scorch marks blotched his cheeks and arms and big, ugly welts had begun to form on his right hand. He looked like he was about to topple over.

"Amos, sit down," I said, rushing to his side.

Gently, I helped him to the ground.

"Wait right here while I fetch some bandages."

Hurrying to the soddy, I gathered some rags, a bottle of Carron oil, a mixture of lime-water and linseed oil used for treating burns, and a bottle of laudanum.

I hurried back to the barn, where I found Amos leaning against the wall, his face racked with pain. He was breathing hard, clutching his right hand in his left hand.

"Here's some laudanum for the pain," I said, kneeling beside him.

Amos turned his head away. "No. The laudanum will make me drowsy. I have to stay awake in case those rustlers come back."

"Okay," I said, setting the bottle aside. "But at least let me treat your burns."

He held out his hand, sucking in deep breaths as I patted Carron oil onto his hand and arm. Grabbing one of the rags, I ripped it into several strips, using them to wrap the burns.

"That should help a bit," I said, sagging down beside him. I was exhausted.

"Thank you," Amos mumbled.

I nodded, then leaned against the wall. My arms and legs had begun to shake as the reality of what had happened slowly sank in.

"You and I could have been killed tonight," I said.

I glanced across the room to Chance who still laid among the ashes and the puddles of blood staining the dirt floor. Scrabbling across the floor on hands and knees, I lifted his limp head and wrapped my arms around his neck. Hugging my dog close, I sobbed.

A faint whimper. I jerked back and looked down. Chance had one eye open.

"Chance!" I cried. "Yer okay!"

Laughing with joy, I hugged him tighter. The dog let out a yap of pain.

"Sorry," I said, releasing him.

"That mutt did a good job tonight," Amos said, struggling to stand. His voice was raspy from the smoke. "Ya done good too, Billy," he added, then turned away.

I didn't know what to say. It was as if the fire had finally made him realize he needed me.

"I'll be in the paddock, guarding the horses fer the rest of the night, just in case those two fools come back," he continued. "You stay here. Keep an eye on the ashes, make sure they don't flare up again."

"Amos!" I called out, stopping him mid-stride. He turned to look at me. "Thanks."

Amos nodded then shuffled off, stooped like an old man.

I retrieved a blanket from one of the stalls then curled up on the ground beside Chance. "I love ya so much," I whispered, trying to hold back the tears.

Chance let out a whine, then thumped his tail.

Despite the pain, I was feeling good. I'd survived. We'd all survived. I no longer felt like a good-fer-nothin. I was good fer something and that made me feel proud.

As I kept watch on the cinders, I thought about what had just happened; the rustlers, the fire, Amos and I working as a team to protect the horses and the stables from harm. I thought about the way we'd saved each other's lives. Tonight, we'd fought a common enemy instead of each other and we'd won.

But something else had happened tonight, something that made a huge difference.

For the first time, Amos had called me Billy.

Chapter Twenty-One

Despite my promise to watch the smoldering ashes, I ended up falling asleep. When I awoke, I felt as though I'd been trampled by a herd of buffalo. Every inch of my body was stiff, my brain still fuzzy from the knock on my head. My eyes burned, gritty from the smoke.

When I tried to sit up, pain stabbed through my back and stomach. Gasping, I flopped back down on the hard dirt floor and pulled up my shirt, smudged with Amos' blood. My belly was blotchy with dark purple bruises.

Chance whined pitifully, scooting closer to me.

"Hey, Chance. How ya feelin' this morning?"

Chance let out a big sigh then laid his head on my chest.

"Yeah, that's pretty much how I feel too."

I snuggled him for a while then slowly rose to my feet. The room suddenly began to spin. Leaning against the wall, I waited for the dizziness to pass then pushed away from the wall. I took one step, then another, hobbling out the back door, into the corral.

The horses were grazing contentedly in the morning sunlight as though nothing had happened. Amos, was nowhere in sight.

Shuffling as fast as my bruised body would allow me, I headed for the soddy. I found Amos, huddled at the table, hunched over a cup of coffee. He'd aged overnight, his face grey and creased. His eyes were slits between swollen lids, his cheeks red and puffy, his nose the size and color of a ripe prune.

It looked impressive. On the table, in front of him, he had placed a crumpled slip of paper, a quill, and a pot of black ink. His right hand was bandaged, snugged close against his chest.

"How's the hand?"

His scowl answered my question. "Terrible. Can't even write a letter to Mr. Slade. I need to tell him about last night's attack."

"I kin write if you'll tell me what to say," I offered.

Amos cleared his throat and ran his tongue across parched lips. Then he turned and glared at me.

"Well, what ya waitin' fer? Git on with it."

Easing myself onto a crate, I glanced at the words Amos had tried to pen. His scribbles were illegible.

"Mr. Slade...," Amos began.

I snatched up the quill, dipped the nib into the bottle of ink, then started writing.

"Last night we were attacked by Dan Saggs and Tom Burrows."

I glanced up in surprise. "Ya know them guys that attacked us?"

Amos let out a snort. Because of his swollen nose, it sounded like a goose honking. He frowned and brushed a hand across his nose, then grimaced. "Sort 'a. Tom's the wretch who worked here fer three weeks. Wouldn't listen, thought he knew better'n me. Gave 'im a piece of my mind. He left madder 'n a bull."

I could understand that. "Ya think he was tryin' to git revenge?"

"Prob'ly."

"What about the guy you called Dan?"

"Tom probably hired 'im," Amos grumbled. "That varmint hooks up with anyone who'll pay 'im to rob, steal, or kill. Man's dumb as a sack 'a nails, but he sure packs a mean wallop!" Amos cringed as he touched his swollen nose.

"Now stop interruptin'. Miller will be here soon and I wanna give 'im this note."

Amos cleared his throat, and I went back to writing. "Chased 'em off for now. Saved horses, some damage to the stables."

Once the letter was finished, I wrapped it in oilcloth, ready for the Pony Express rider.

"Yer gonna have to help me saddle Aurora," Amos mumbled with a fierce scowl.

I was shocked. This was a first. The man had to be in a great deal of pain to ask for help twice in one morning.

I headed out to the barn with Amos shuffling slowly behind. I gathered the necessary equipment, then fetched Thunder from the corral. He was an ornery horse on good days but after last night's fire, he would probably even more unruly. I wasn't feeling too great myself so tacking him up was a struggle from the start.

"Would ya hold still," I grumbled, fastening the cinch.

"Gonna need to tighten that," Amos muttered.

Scowling, I tightened it one notch, then lowered the stirrup.

After sliding the reins over his neck, I tried to insert the bit into Thunder's mouth. He didn't want to open up. I gently pushed my thumb into the toothless gap between his jaws which forced him to open his mouth.

Quickly, I slid the bit in then lifted the crown piece over his ears.

"Gonna spook the horse, fighting with 'im like that," Amos grumbled.

I pressed my lips together to avoid spewing angry words. I was still tightening the chin strap when I heard the *thrump, thrump, thrump* of Miller's horse. Ebony tore into the station as though her tail were on fire, kicking up clods of dirt in her wake. Hauling on the reins, Miller pulled the mare to a halt. The poor animal was heaving and dripping with sweat.

"Gee, Amos!" Miller exclaimed, as he slid out of the saddle. "That there's one of the biggest shiners I ever seen. Kid finally git even?" He winked at me, and we both burst into laughter.

"Keep yer nonsense to yerself," Amos snapped, handing Miller the note. "Be sure these gits to Slade right quick. It's important."

"Sure thing." He unlocked one of the pockets on the Mochila, then slid the note in and locked it again. Then he slid the mail bag off his horse, flung it over Thunder's saddle, and flung himself up into the saddle.

Like an arrow shot from a bow, Thunder sped out of the station. Horse and rider crested the hill then disappeared.

"See to Ebony, will ya?" Amos said, then turned around and vomited on the ground. "Come git me if ya need anythin.' I'm going back to bed."

Chapter Twenty-Two

It took most of the day to clean up the damage caused by the fire. I could tell Amos was in a lot of pain even though he tried not to show it.

"Why don't ya send a note with Miller or Clyde, askin' for a doctor to come out," I said.

"Don't need no doctor," Amos growled. "It'll just take time."

Chance was hurting too. He spent most of his time sleeping. When he was awake, he drifted from one spot to another, tail tucked between his legs.

I tried my best to ignore my own aches and pains but was thankful when the day's work was finally done, and I could go to bed.

Within a couple of days, Chance and I were back to normal. At least my body was. But inside, I was still on edge, wondering if the rustlers might come back. I had a nasty feeling our troubles weren't over. Every shadow, every strange sound, made my heart skip a beat. I slept fitfully too, waking at the slightest noise.

Several days later, my uneasiness proved correct. Amos and I were in the yard, waiting on Clyde. Ebony was saddled and ready, but Clyde hadn't arrived yet.

"Must be running late," I said, as Amos paced nervously back and forth across the yard. But deep down, I feared the worst.

Plenty of dangers lurked out there, waiting for lone riders; rustlers, bandits, wild animals. Just recently, one of the Pony Express riders had gone missing in Nevada. The horse showed up at one of the stations, but its rider was never found.

At last, we heard the thump of hooves pounding the earth. In the dim light of a half moon, I could see the silhouette of a horse cresting the rim of the hill. Thunder galloped down the well-trodden path, dripping with sweat, ribs heaving with every labored breath.

His nostrils were dilated, the muscles in his neck twitching from exhaustion. Clyde lay sprawled over the horse's neck, his tousled head drooping dangerously to one side.

"Clyde!" I called out as Amos caught the reins with his good hand. He pulled the horse to a stop. With a sickening thud, Clyde toppled off the horse, landing on the packed dirt.

I noticed the blood immediately; blood on the saddle, blood on the horse, blood on the ground. Thunder didn't appear to be wounded, so where was all this blood coming from?

Dropping to my knees, I slid an arm under Clyde's head. "What happened?".

Clyde tried to sit up but the effort was too much. With a groan, he slumped back against my arm. Those few seconds were enough for me to see the red stain on the back of his shirt.

"Two... ambush... creek," Clyde mumbled.

"Ya git a look at 'em?" Amos asked.

"Pony...tail... burns...face...," Clyde muttered.

Amos shot me a meaningful look. I understood it clearly. Tom and Dan were still out there.

"Let's git ya inside," Amos said, dropping Thunder's reins.

A spasm of pain crossed Amos' face as he bent to help Clyde to his feet. Wobbling dangerously, the two men staggered forward, listing to the right. Rushing forward, I wrapped an arm around Clyde's waist.

Between the three of us, we managed a few steps before Clyde's legs buckled. I quickly grabbed the man's britches, half-walking, half-carrying him into the soddy.

"Lay 'im on my bunk."

"The back of his shirt has blood on it," I said, my hand coming away soaked with warm blood.

"Lay 'im on his side, then."

I nodded grimly.

As soon as Clyde was on the bed, Amos tore off his bloodied shirt, revealing a bright, red hole where a bullet had entered his back. It troubled me when I saw how fast Clyde's blood welled from the wound and seeped down his back and onto the bed.

"Heat some water and grab some rags," Amos snapped.

Dragging a crate over to the bed, he sat down, then pressed Clyde's shirt against the wound. "We've got to stop him from bleeding out."

Hurrying to the stove where the kettle was still warm from supper, I poured the water into a bucket, added a bit of cold water, then snatched up several feed sacks lying in a corner.

Setting the bucket on the floor near the bed, I started ripping the sacks into strips. Snatching the first one from my hand, Amos dunked it in the warm water, wrung it out with one hand, then pressed it against the raw wound on Clyde's back.

I'd expected Clyde to wince or cry out in pain, but he was silent as a stone. He'd passed out.

"He gonna make it?" I whispered, watching Amos struggle to stop the bleeding.

"Ain't too sure," Amos scowled. This was the first time I'd seen him so upset. "Wound's bigger'n I thought. He needs a doc."

Glancing at Clyde's pale face, I remembered the first time we'd met. He'd been so cocky and carefree. Tears pooled in my eyes. I couldn't stand by and watch him die. I had to do something.

"I'll fetch a doc," I blurted out.

Amos tossed the rag on the floor. It was wet through with blood. "Quit yer foolish talk and hand me another rag," he said, gruffly.

"I'm serious, Amos," I insisted, passing him a second cloth. "Ain't there a doc near Scott's Bluff?"

"Sure. But there's one little snag."

"What?"

"Ya don't know how to git there."

"No, but Ebony does. She's been to Scott's Bluff and back 'nough times to know the route. 'sides, the mail's still gotta be delivered."

"Be better if I go," Amos persisted. "Least I know how to…"

"Ya can't ride!" I broke in. "Yer hurt too bad."

Amos' face reddened with anger. He rose to his feet, knocking over the bucket of water in the process. Red-stained water seeped across the floor.

I tried to convince him another way. "Besides, yer needed here to protect the station and took care 'a Clyde. Who does that leave?"

Amos glowered, then glanced at the man lying on his bed. He had very little choice.

"It's risky," he mumbled under his breath. But I could tell he was starting to waver.

"Lemme go, Amos. Please. I can do it."

Amos rubbed his neck as he paced the floor, mulling over what he should do, smearing blood on his shirt collar in the process. "Go on then," he grunted, waving a hand dismissively.

"Yes!" I cried out, punching the air.

"Don't git too excited. Gonna be a long, hard ride, 'specially in the dark."

Reaching under his bunk, he pulled out a Colt revolver and holster. "Ya know how to shoot one of these things?"

A lump formed in my throat as I looked at the revolver. "Do... do I need one?"

Amos handed me the holster. "Might not, but ya never can tell. Beasts and bandits, a plenty out there."

My hands were trembling so much, I was having a hard time buckling the holster around my waist. Snugging it as tight as I could around my narrow hips, I held out my hand for the revolver.

Amos laid it in my palm. It was heavier and bulkier than I'd thought. Gingerly, I slid the weapon into the holster, praying I wouldn't have to use it. I headed to the door then paused for a second. I turned to look at Amos.

"Thanks, Amos. Ya won't be sorry ya trusted me."

Amos stared at me, hard. "Jus'... jus' come back alive."

With a quick nod, I ran out into the night. Thunder was waiting in the yard. I led him to the corral. With water in the trough, he would be all right until Amos could tend to him.

Transferring the Mochila onto Ebony's saddle, I swung up onto her back and shoved my feet into the stirrups. Chance ran circles around the horse, barking and carrying on. Looking down at Chance him, I realized just how tall Ebony was.

"Stay here and protect Amos," I told Chance.

Chance cocked his head to one side then laid down in front of the soddy door. He looked so sad; it broke my heart. "I'll be back. I promise."

I turned the mare's head about. With a burst of speed that nearly threw me from the saddle, Ebony hurtled into the dark night.

I let out a whoop of excitement.

"Yee-ha!"

At last, all those long months of working and waiting had paid off. I was finally carrying the mail for the Pony Express.

Chapter Twenty-Three

Hunching my upper body snuggly against Ebony's neck, I focused on becoming one with this force of nature as we blazed over hillocks and across grassy fields in a blur of speed. There was no slowing her down, no stopping her now.

The reins were useless. I had no need to lead her. Ebony knew where she was going. While I had a vague idea of the route, thanks to the map posted in the barn, Ebony knew every dip and rise and turn.

Overhead, a fickle moon teased us. At times, it slipped behind a veil of clouds, enveloping us in darkness. Then, unexpectedly, it would break through, casting strange and eerie shadows across our path.

I sat up straighter in the saddle, increasingly aware of the night around me. Wild calls and frightening noises filled the dark night, sending my heart racing in rhythm with Ebony's galloping hooves. I grew uneasy as I thought about Clyde.

Tree toads trilled in the darkness; I briefly wondered if it might be thieves sending a signal to each other as they hid along my path. Could that hoot be a rustlers' call, not an owl? Each cry was a possible threat, every shadow a potential foe. I felt vulnerable, exposed, as though hundreds of eyes were watching me, ready to pounce.

Despite the possible dangers, I was giddy with joy. Being able to ride Ebony and deliver the mail sent a thrill deep down inside me. I would happily spend the rest of my life in the saddle. All I had to do now was convince Mr. Slade.

Then out of the night came a frightening sound.

A-woooo

Wolves!

A-woooo

Fear gripped me like a vise around my chest.

A-woooo

The howls were growing stronger and louder.

All at once, I caught a glimpse of grey as a massive wolf burst out of the shadows. Its amber eyes glowed in the dusky moonlight like hungry flames. A loud rumble rose from its chest, feral and chilling. Within seconds, masses of grey fur came at us from every direction, hulking brutes, strong, fast, and fierce.

We are going to die, I thought, reaching for my revolver. *We are going to die.* Every part of me was shaking. *We are going to die.*

A grey blur lunged at Ebony, nipping the soft flesh above her ankle. She screamed, then reared. Leaning into her neck to keep my balance, I wrapped one arm around the horse's neck. With the other hand, I raised the gun then fired into the pack. A scream broke through the air. I'd done it! I had struck one of them!

Ebony's front legs hit the ground with a force that jarred my back and knocked the wind out of me, then she put on a tremendous burst of speed. Before I could catch my breath, Ebony had outrun the hungry wolves.

I shuddered at the thought of what could have happened. My hands were shaking so much, it took three tries to slide the revolver back into its holster. Leaning tightly against Ebony's neck, I breathed a prayer of thanks that the Overland Express had bought the fastest and sturdiest horses. Anything less and we would both be dead.

As the miles stretched on, I relaxed a little, settling into Ebony's steady rhythm. I tried to forget about the wolves and bring back the excitement of the ride. My thoughts turned to Clyde.

My throat tightened at the thought of losing him. I didn't know him well, but he was always a bright light on those dreary days when he rode through our station. I thought of Chance, of the promise I'd made to him and to Amos that I would return. I hoped I could keep my promise.

In the distance, I noticed a flash of lightening and realized how quiet it was. I held my breath, listening hard. Other than the pounding of Ebony's hooves, the night was eerily silent. Those sounds which had previously spooked me were gone now.

No chirps. No hoots. No insects chatter.

The silence could only mean one thing; a nasty storm was brewing. A breeze kicked up, swelling to a gusty wind, gathering strength as it swooshed across the vast, open land. Without trees to break some of the wind's strength, it whipped at my clothes and stung my face.

A fine drizzle set in, quickly thickening into a downpour. Worry turned to fear as lightening ripped through the clouds and thunder rumbled across the sky.

Zap!

A jagged flash gouged the sky. I felt myself going cold as I realized how defenseless we were against the storm.

Boom!

Thunder growled back.

Zap!

Any minute, we could be struck dead.

Boom!

Bolt after bolt struck the ground with thunder hard on its heels, slamming into the earth with powerful force. A few feet to our left, lightning struck a sage brush. It burst into flames. Ebony reared, letting out a shrill cry of terror then bolted as though pursued by a prairie fire. I clung to her neck, terrified.

Then gradually, the storm dwindled to a gentle rain. A hush spread across the land. Ebony slowed to a canter. Her flanks were heaving. I worried she'd exhausted all her energy.

"That was close," I panted. "Much too close."

Chapter Twenty-Four

Within minutes, I heard Pumpkin Creek. As we drew near, the rumble of the swollen stream grew louder. The creek had swollen from the recent downpour, its current swift and strong.

Stay on the horse, I told myself. *Stay on the horse at all costs.*

Cautiously, Ebony ventured into the creek. Frigid water seeped over the tops of my boots, drenching my socks, turning my feet into blocks of ice. I shivered, no longer giddy with excitement, but from the chilly water. I was cold and wet and miserable.

Ebony seemed to be struggling with the current. We'd nearly reached the opposite bank where she could touch the bottom when she lost her footing. She stumbled, pitching me into the icy water. I landed hard on the jagged rocks lining the bottom of the creek.

Clutching the reins in a life-or-death grip, I scrambled to my feet. The mare scrabbled for shore, tugging me onto the riverbank where I collapsed, exhausted. Sprawled on the sharp rocks, I was unaware of the water lapping at my feet. I closed my eyes, thankful to have made it to the opposite bank, yet longing for just a few moments of sleep. I was so tired, so dreadfully tired.

Ebony wouldn't let me sleep. She kept nudging me, urging me to stand up. With a groan, I rolled onto all fours then pushed to my feet. In the darkness, it was hard to see where I was walking. My foot struck a rock. I tripped, falling hard on a sharp rock.

"Ouch!" I cried out, rubbing my knee.

Instead of standing back up, I bent double, using my feet and hands to scrabble up the bank. At the top of the riverbank, I drew myself up and dragged myself back into the saddle, drenched and humbled.

Perhaps Pa was right. Perhaps I was a good-for-nothin', conceited fool. How could I have thought I was strong enough or smart enough to manage the ride to Scott's Bluff?

As we took off again, I noticed Ebony was faltering. She'd become sluggish, her flanks heaving, her gait heavy and uneven.

"Can't be much further," I said, patting her shoulder. "Come on, let's finish this run."

The soothing words seemed to help for she broke into a canter. Shivering, I settled back into the saddle, trying to ignore the pain. My drenched clothing, so heavy with the weight of all the water it had soaked up, pressed on my neck, my back, my shoulders.

My hands were stiff with cold... I could barely hold on. My toes....

With a burst of energy that caught me by surprise, Ebony suddenly surged forward. Squinting into the darkness, I noticed a faint light twinkling up ahead. This had to be Scott's Bluff!

"We did it!" I cheered. "We did it!"

With a shaky laugh, I patted Ebony's neck. "Good job, Ebony."

As soon as we rode into the yard, a large man rushed out of the house to meet us.

"Howdy," he called, grabbing hold of Ebony's reins. "Name's Big Joe. Where's Clyde?"

"Mud Springs…" My brain was so muddled, I was finding it hard to speak. "He was shot."

"Is he dead?" he asked, his eyes growing wide.

"No… but he's in pretty bad shape."

Big Joe dropped the reins, ran across the yard, and burst into the house. I stumbled after him, struggling to place one foot in front of the other.

"Hank, mail's here," Big Joe told one of the two men sitting beside the hearth.

Immediately, Hank leaped to his feet and rushed out into the dark night.

"John," Big Joe addressed the second man, "fetch the doc and send him to Mud Springs. Tell him Clyde's been shot."

Without a word, John also jumped up and hurried out the door.

Turning back to me, Big Joe smiled and clapped his huge hand on my shoulder. "So, who are you?"

"Billy. I work at Mud Springs station."

"Oh, sure," Big Joe said. "Clyde's told us about ya."

"He has?"

"Sure. Come warm yerself by the fire while the missus fixes ya some stewed apples and a hot cup 'a coffee."

All I wanted was a bed. Heck, I'd settle for some quiet corner where I could curl up and sleep. Instead, I followed Big Joe to a large fireplace. I sank into a chair, stretching my legs in front of the crackling fire. Laying my head back, I closed my eyes, soaking in the warmth.

I heard Big Joe tell someone to tend to my horse, then he plopped down on a chair across from me. "Tell me what happened."

His voice sounded so far away. I struggled to keep my eyes open but the chill and extreme exhaustion had taken their toll. Next thing I knew, someone was shaking me, gently but firmly.

It was Big Joe, standing over me. "Tired?"

Tired? Tired didn't even come close. I simply nodded.

"There's a cot up there ya can use," he said, pointing to a loft. "If ya toss down yer wet clothes, the missus will wash 'em."

I glanced down at myself, suddenly realizing what a filthy, wretched mess I was. Struggling not to wince, I stood, then tottered across the room, staggering up the ladder to the loft. Peeling off my clothes, I dropped them to the floor below.

Gratefully, I sank onto the cot and covered myself with the buffalo robe lying at the foot of the bed.

Before I could even enjoy the sweet comfort of a soft, warm bed, I fell asleep.

Chapter Twenty-Five

Raised voices broke through my dreams, waking me from a pleasant sleep. For a moment, my groggy mind couldn't figure out where I was. Then the wild and fearful events of the previous day came rushing back. I shivered at the memories then snuggled deeper under the buffalo robe.

"Oh, let him sleep," a woman's voice exclaimed. "Poor boy's all tuckered out."

"He needs to get up," a deep baritone argued. "Day's a wastin'."

Heavy footsteps thumped up the ladder. Big Joe's smiling face popped into view. Placing a washbowl on the wooden floor along with my clean clothes, he gave me a big smile.

"Howdy," he said. "Sleep well?"

I nodded.

"Bessie's cookin' breakfast. Figured you'd wanna head back by daylight."

"Thanks," I said, as Big Joe climbed back down.

Reluctantly, I pushed back the covers and stood, cringing with pain. My whole body felt battered and bruised. I groaned at the thought of getting back in the saddle. What I really wanted to do was go back to bed. Instead, I slowly stretched, working the stiffness, then knelt beside the basin to wash myself.

Dipping my hands into the water, I was surprised to find out the water was warm. What a special treat! I washed my face then dabbed at my wounds. It was slow and painful because I'd skinned myself up so badly.

I dressed, wincing as the clothes rubbed against my sores, cinched the holster around my waist. I hoped I wouldn't have to use it the on the ride back to Mud Springs. Gingerly, I climbed down the ladder.

"Mornin'," Bessie greeted me with a cheerful voice, a sunny smile, and a plate piled high with food. "Sleep well?"

I nodded timidly.

"Sit down," she said, setting the plate on the table. It was heaped with plump sausages, scrambled eggs, stewed apples, and fresh-baked bread slathered with butter and blackberry jam.

"Let me know if ya need anythin' else."

I tucked in, enjoying every bite. Why couldn't Mr. Slade have sent me here instead of Mud Springs?

"So," Bessie said, sitting down across from me. "What happened to Clyde?"

She tisked and tutted as I told her about the ambush, his injuries, and my offer to carry the mail.

"Poor boy," she said, swiping at a tear. "I hope he makes it."

I thought about the mother I'd never known. Her face was nothing more than a vague copy of my own. From now on, Bessie's face would come to mind when I thought of my mother.

All too soon, I'd finished my breakfast. It was time to head back to Amos and Mud Springs station. "Thank ya fer breakfast," I said. "And the clean clothes."

"Yer welcome," she said, tucking two oatmeal cookies in my coat pocket. She smiled and patted my cheek. "In case ya get hungry on yer way home."

I felt my face grow warm. I dipped my chin then walked out. I was anxious to see how Ebony was doing. As I entered the stables, several horses stuck their heads out of their stalls. I stroked each one as I made my way down the passageway, looking for Ebony. Where was Ebony? Was she too injured to even stand at her door to greet me?

A black nose suddenly popped over a stall door, followed by a black muzzle and a silky black mane. I let out a breath of relief as I rushed towards her.

"Mornin' Ebony," I said, reaching up to scratch her head. "Glad to see yer up and movin'."

I opened the gate and entered Ebony's stall. The mare laid her chin on my shoulder as I stroked her silky mane.

"Ready to go home?"

Ebony nickered.

"Billy!" a voice boomed behind me.

I jumped. Big Joe stood in the doorway.

"Did my Bessie fix ya some breakfast?" he asked, setting down the bucket of oats he was carrying.

I patted my stomach. "Yes, sir."

Big Joe laughed. "She's a mighty fine cook, ain't she?"

"The best."

"Good thing, too," Big Joe went on, "'cause I'm a mighty fine eater." He rubbed his rounded belly. "You two ready to leave?"

"I'm hopin' to but is Ebony up to it?"

"Bah, she's fine. Cleaned her up really good and rubbed some cream on her sores. By the way, how did she get that bite?"

I quickly told him about the wolves and our ordeal with Pumpkin Creek. Big Joe frowned, tutted, and whistled as I told him about last night's adventure.

"Sure, hope ya have a better trip home," he said, tacking her up.

He led Ebony out to the yard where I gingerly mounted her. "Thank ya fer everything."

"Anytime," Big Joe answered.

With a click of my tongue, Ebony shot out of the station, streaking across the golden fields as though yesterday's mishaps hadn't even happened. The trip was so much easier in the daylight. I even had the chance to see the great rock formations of Scott's Bluff rising sharply on our left as we rushed past, the Platte River running alongside it, amber meadows stretching as far as the eye could see.

The view was breathtaking. For a moment, I simply enjoyed the thrilling ride. To the east, a lone spire rose from the brown earth like a finger pointing to the heavens. According to the map in the stables at Mud Springs, this was Chimney Rock.

Soon afterwards, I spotted Courthouse Rock and Jailhouse Rock, an impressive pair of stone bluffs looming boldly against the bright blue sky. They looked so forlorn in this vast, open stretch of land. I remembered Amos telling me these landmarks were a halfway marker for pioneers travelling west. From here on out, they would be leaving the plains behind as they ventured into the rugged mountains.

"Missed all this last night," I said to Ebony as we whooshed past.

As Ebony settled into a steady rhythm, I relaxed into the saddle. I wondered what was happening back at Mud Springs. Had the doctor arrived in time to save Clyde? Had the authorities caught Tom and Dan? What about Amos? How was he managing?

My thoughts turned to Chance. I remembered the miserable look on his face as I rode off without him. Did he understand I would be coming home? I frowned. Home? Where had that word come from?

Soon, the babble of Pumpkin Creek greeted us. This morning, the water was calmer, though the swift-flowing stream still churned between its banks. My heart clenched with worry as she inched down the slippery bank. This time, Ebony crossed the creek without any trouble while I held my feet high to keep them dry. We clambered up the far side, nearly reaching the top, when Ebony snagged her foot in a muddle of tree roots lining the bank. Her knees buckled and she came crashing down, toppling like a felled tree.

Chapter Twenty-Six

I tried to jump clear as Ebony fell but I wasn't fast enough. Ebony tumbled onto my right foot, pinning it under her body.

I let out a blood-curdling scream.

"Get off! Get off!"

My foot was trapped in the stirrup, Ebony's full weight crushing it into the ground. Black spots danced on the edge of my vision. For a moment, I could barely focus and thought I might pass out.

"Get off!" I gasped, struggling to push the massive weight off me.

Failing like a turtle on its back, Ebony pedaled the air. As she rocked onto her side, I swiftly yanked my foot free. Ebony scrambled to her feet while I laid on the ground, sucking in deep breaths. The right side of my head, my right arm, and my shoulder throbbed painfully where they'd been slammed into the ground. But it was my ankle that worried me the most.

Slowly, I rolled to my knees, groaning as the world span around. Sucking in a few deep breaths, I waited for the dizziness to stop then staggered to my feet, letting out another yelp as I placed weight on my injured foot.

Ebony appeared mostly unharmed by the fall, yet she favored her front right leg. If I rode her home, I could possibly aggravate her injury. A lame horse was worthless and was typically shot. I didn't want to run that risk.

"What are we going to do?" I said, burying my face in Ebony's thick black mane.

Ebony nickered.

"I don't wanna walk on this sore foot, but I sure don't want to risk your life by riding ya all the way home."

Most riders would have remounted the horse without thought for its injuries. But for me, Ebony was more than just a means to get from one place to another. She was my friend.

Glancing left and right, I tried to come up with an idea. Nearby, several branches lay on the ground. Suddenly, a plan began to take form in my mind; if I could find one solid enough to support my weight, I could use it as a crutch. I glanced over the sticks and picked the sturdiest looking one, hoping it would hold up until we got home.

Sucking in a deep breath, I sat down and tugged off my boot. Beads of sweat broke out on my forehead as I fought off a fresh wave of nausea. The ankle was swollen and had already turned purplish-blue. I didn't think it was broken but expected it would hurt for a quite a while.

Ripping two strips of cloth from my shirt, I wrapped them around my ankle to give some support, then pulled my boot back on. I bit my bottom lip to stifle a yelp, worried I might draw wolves with my cries. Tiny droplets of blood trickled down my lip then down my chin, landing on my hand.

With the help of Ebony's saddle and leaning fully on my left foot, I pulled myself up. Tentatively, I placed some weight on my right foot, letting out a small whimper. The ankle was throbbing, yet the pain was no longer so brutal.

"Looks like we're gonna have to hobble home together, Ebony. Jus' hope the wolves are sleepin' off a good meal and will leave us alone."

Standing was harder than I'd thought. I swayed, trying to find my balance, struggling with the crude ankle brace and crutch. My head hurt something awful. Dizziness hit every time I turned my head to the left or the right. But I had to get home, and this was the only way it was going to happen.

Ebony and I stumbled up the bank. Though my foot throbbed, I pressed on.

One footstep, then another.

Everything hurt. My head was pounding, my shoulder throbbing in rhythm with my footsteps.

Thump, thump, thump.

Beside me, Ebony plodded on, her limp growing more noticeable.

"Hang on, Ebony," I said, pulling on her reins.

Ripping another two strips of cloth from my shirt, I wrapped them snuggly around the bottom of her leg, just above the hoof.

"Ok, let's go. Let's show Amos we're braver and stronger than he thinks we are."

Slowly, we trudged up another hill. Before us lay nothing but endless fields flecked with sweet clover.

Keep moving, I reminded myself over and over, despite the stabbing pain. If we wanted to live, to survive the dangers lurking everywhere, we had to keep moving.

Weariness dragged at me as we wound our way down into the valley, then up the next hill. My legs were heavy, as though weights had been tied to them. Each step was harder and more painful than the one before.

Something moved up on the hilltop in front of us.

Pulling Ebony to a stop, I reached for my revolver, my gaze trained on the blurry shape up ahead. Another one came to stand beside the first, then another. I felt the hairs on my neck stand on end as the numbers grew. Beside me, Ebony shuffled restlessly.

The shapes slowly turned their heads. They'd heard us. If these were wolves, we were dead. As their heads pointed in our direction, I noticed the horns. I let out the breath I didn't realize I'd been holding.

"Not wolves," I said, sagging against Ebony. "Just a herd of antelope."

Slipping my weapon back into its sheath, I began the steep climb to the top of the hill. The wind had picked up. Buttoning my jacket, I pressed on, determined to reach home before nightfall.

The haunting memory of our encounter with the wolves was like a goad at my back, pushing me onward even when the pain was at its worst.

On the western horizon, streaks of russet and gold stretched across the sky. Soon, night would descend. Just as the last rays of daylight were fading, we crested another hill much like all the others.

My heart lurched. Below us, a dark shape stood out, mired in the muddy dip between two hills; though nothing but a shack, it was the most beautiful sight in the world.

Slumping against Ebony, I let myself cry. Tears of happiness. Tears of relief. I'd survived. No, we'd survived. We'd made it home. *Home.*

A strange word. A confusing word. A simple word, yet it embraced so much.

Ebony nickered loudly.

"Happy to be home?" I whispered, stroking her neck. "Well, come on then. Let's finish this run."

Out of the gloom, a bundle of fur came barreling up the hill towards us, ears flopping, tail wagging, and barking wildly.

"Chance!"

I stooped, cringing with pain, as Chance dashed into my open arms, knocking me to the ground. Standing over me, Chance slobbered all over my face, licking my nose, my cheek, my ear, then my nose again.

"Missed ya too," I laughed, struggling to push him away. "Come on, let me git up."

I finally managed to shove him off. I struggled to stand, leaning heavily on Ebony. With the faint glow of candlelight to strengthen and guide us, Ebony and I limped into Mud Springs.

The soddy door flew open. Amos' bulky frame filled the doorway. "Expected ya much sooner." But the smile on his face belied his gruff tone.

"Ebony tripped on a tree root. We had to walk part of the way," I said, struggling to keep Chance away from my sore ankle. "How's Clyde?"

"Mendin'," Amos answered. "Go on in. I'll tend to Ebony."

Gratefully, I surrendered the reins then ducked into the soddy. The air was thick with the smell of blood and ointment. A pile of soiled rags laid beside the door. Yet even this unpleasantness couldn't dampen my good mood.

Clyde huddled beside the stove, a large bandage wrapped around his chest, a thin blanket draped across his bare shoulders. He was hunched over, staring off into space, his large hands wrapped around a cup of coffee. His face, pale and drawn, looked as though he'd aged several years.

Easing down onto one of the crates, I slid my boot off, cringing with pain.

"Well, look what the wind blew in," Clyde said, shifting, then wincing as he angled his body to look at me. "Glad to see ya back safe and sound."

"Well… safe at least," I said, propping my sore foot on another crate. "How ya feelin'?"

"Some better," Clyde answered. "Thanks, fer fetchin' the doc. Ya prob'ly saved my life."

"You'd 'a done the same fer me."

Amos entered, stomping his feet. He looked worn and frail, his nose swollen and purple as a wild plum, eyes enclosed by puffy scarlet bruises. His right hand, swathed in a rag, was coddled protectively against his chest.

"Weathers turned chilly," he said, poking the fire. Tossing another log into the stove, he stirred it into a bright blaze.

"Will Ebony be, okay?" I asked, worried.

"She'll be right as rain once her ankle heals. Ya did good not riding her."

I smiled, grateful for his kind words. I was feeling rather proud of myself. I'd proved I was not a good-for-nothin' like Pa kept tellin' me. Right now, I felt like I could do just about anything.

Amos slowly lowered himself onto a crate. "So, Billy, tell us what happened."

I told them.

I told them about the wolf I shot, causing the pack to flee. I told them about the storm. I told them about Pumpkin Creek, swollen from the rain, and how I swam across swift-flowing waters. I was bending the truth a little, but I was aching to hear someone to tell me I was brave, smart, and good for something.

"So how did Ebony git hurt?" Amos said, lines creasing his brow.

I shrugged. "Some ol' tree root tripped her up."

"Sounds like a scary adventure," Clyde said. "Good job, Billy."

I smiled, feeling just a little bit proud of myself. I just hoped Ebony wouldn't snitch on me and tell them how scared I truly was.

Chapter Twenty-Seven

The large, grey wolf had pinned me to the ground, its evil yellow eyes just inches from my face. His massive jaws opened, baring formidable white teeth sharp as knives. His breath was hot and rancid.

Though I struggled to fight him off, I couldn't move.

This is it. It's over. I'm going to die.

The beast's coarse wet tongue grazed my cheek. I screamed.

My eyes snapped open as the sound of my own shrieks jolted me awake. Towering over me loomed the beast of my dreams.

"Chance!" Ya scared me!"

Chance licked my nose, my chin, my cheeks, covering my face with wet, slobbery drool.

"Enough," I laughed, raising my arm to push him away, then gasped as pain seared through my arm and shoulder.

Chance barked happily, not understanding why I wasn't jumping up to open the door for him.

"Okay, okay," I groaned.

I struggled to stand, then sank back onto my straw bed as pain shot through my foot and ankle, all the way up to my knee. A dull pain pulsed at my temple where my head had smacked against the ground. Reaching up, I felt a tender lump just beneath the skin.

Pushing myself up onto my good leg, I hopped to the door. Chance dashed out, paused just a second to sniff the air, then scurried off after some scent.

Grabbing my crutch, I hobbled across the yard and into the soddy. Amos was asleep at the table, his head resting on his arms. His injured hand, still wrapped in a rag, rested on his lap. Clyde was fast asleep on the lower bunk, Amos' buffalo robe tucked around him.

In the stove, red-orange embers gave off a faint glow. I built up the fire, stirring up the flagging cinders, then added a couple of logs. Soon, I had a nice fire going.

Then, I set about cooking breakfast. With only one good foot to stand on, it took a while. It was slow, painstakingly slow. But I couldn't ask Amos and Clyde to help. They were worse off than I was. Limping out to the rain barrel, I collected water for coffee, then stumbled back into the house, plopping the kettle onto the stove with a loud *clank*.

Amos yawned, stretched, then rose unsteadily to his feet. He tried to flex his swollen fingers but winced. Reaching for his jacket, he shuffled out the door, slamming it shut behind him.

I let out a sigh. Somehow, I'd expected things to be different after my two-day absence. But nothing had changed. Except for his kind words about the way I'd cared for Ebony, Amos was still as grumpy as ever.

Seconds later, a terrible roar carried across the yard. Chance started barking furiously, just as he had the night Dan and Tom had shown up. Heart racing, I grabbed the rifle hanging over the door and rushed out in a painful, faltering run.

Fearing the worst, I hobbled as quickly as I could across the yard. I peered around the door of the barn. Amos's face was contorted with pain as he cradled his injured hand against his chest. Aurora cowered in a corner, halfway saddled and snorting nervously. Her eyes were wide with fear.

"Ain't got time fer this nonsense," Amos growled.

With a fierce kick, he sent a bucket flying across the barn. It barely missed my head.

"Whoa!" I cried out.

Amos spun around. "Go away!" he snapped.

"Thought fer sure you was bein' attacked by some savage animal, the way you was hollerin' and carryin' on," I said.

Before Amos could throw something at me, I snatched up the bridle laying on the ground then limped up to the frightened mare.

"Shhh!" I whispered softly. "Ain't you he's mad at."

Scratching Aurora behind the ears, I slid the bridle over her head. Behind me, Amos was stomping back and forth, mumbling under his breath. I ignored him as I continued to tack the horse.

"Is Miller due today?" I asked.

"Nah. Clyde's gonna need her," Amos grumbled.

"What?" I yelled, frightening the poor mare again. "He ain't fit to ride!"

"Work don't stop jus' 'cause yer hurtin' a bit," Amos snapped.

Deep anger surged through me. "Seems to me he's hurtin' a whole lot more 'n a bit."

"Ain't my choice neither," Amos yelled. "But Slade wants 'im back on the job. Now if yer gonna butt in and take over my job, then ya better quit jawin' and git that bag 'a nerves saddled."

Seething, I limped into the tack room and yanked a saddle off the workbench. When I returned, I found Amos running his good hand under the cheek straps.

"Need to tighten this," he fussed.

I rolled my eyes as I lifted the saddle onto the mare's back. I was about to fasten the girth when Amos yelled, "not that one!"

Startled, Aurora backed away from him, wedging me against the back wall.

"Dern it, Amos," I shouted. I was tired of his outbursts. "Do ya have to yell so loud? I already got one bad foot, so I don't need Aurora stepping on the other because ya spooked her with all yer hollerin'."

Amos glowered at me, then lowered his voice. "Stirrup's loose on that saddle. I need to fix it first."

I muscled the mare away from me then squeezed past to fetch another saddle. I returned with a different saddle and lifted it onto the horse's back.

"This one, okay?" I asked, peevishly.

Amos nodded. I fastened the girth.

"Not that tight…," Amos began.

I snapped. "Amos! I know what I'm doin'."

Fuming, I led the horse into the yard, hitched her to a post, then stormed into the soddy.

As I turned to close the door, I saw Amos lifted a stirrup, check the cinch, then drop it back down.

"Stubborn ol' coot," I grumbled.

"Amos drivin' ya crazy?"

I swung around to find Clyde sitting on the edge of the bunk, his face drained of color, his hair a wild mess of ginger curls.

"Amos seems to think he's the only one knows how to saddle a horse," I muttered.

"Bah, don't pay him no mind," Clyde said. "He just likes to be sure his riders don't git hurt slidin' off a loose saddle."

Clyde slowly rose, swaying alarmingly to the left then the right. I limped over just as he sank back down onto the bed.

"How does Slade think yer gonna ride when ya can hardly stand?" I asked.

"I'm… fine," Clyde said, wincing. "Mail must be delivered on time…" His voice sounded amazingly like Mr. Slade's.

I chuckled. "Ya sound jus' like 'im."

"And yer sounding more and more like Amos," Clyde teased.

"Am not!" I argued, horrified at the idea.

Clyde slowly stood, bracing against one of the bunk's supports. I had to stop myself from reaching out to help. Instead, I hobbled to the stove, then grabbed a rag to lift the kettle.

Slowly, Clyde shuffled across the room, easing onto a crate like an old man. He sat still for a moment, trying to catch his breath while watching me fix breakfast.

"You two act like ya hate each other, but that ol' coot out there…," Clyde cocked a thumb towards the door, "… he sure does care 'bout ya."

My head jerked up. "No, he don't."

"Well, he sure seemed worried 'bout ya the whole time you was gone. Wouldn't sit still. Kept pacin' back and forth, drivin' me plum crazy. When he wasn't pacin', he was outside, hackin' at the wood with one hand."

"Prob'ly worried 'bout Ebony," I snorted, picking up the container of salt. Measuring a small amount into my palm, I tossed it into the cornmeal, whisking it a little harder than necessary.

"Hey, I'm just tellin' ya what I saw. But Amos sure seems relieved yer back."

I didn't know what to say. His words left me feeling surprised and awkward.

After breakfast, Amos and I somehow got Clyde into the saddle then sent him on his way. Slouching dangerously to one side, the poor lad looked more like a ragamuffin than the proud messenger we'd always known. I just hoped Clyde would make it to Scott's Bluff. Bessie would feed and nurse him back to health.

She was good at that.

Chapter Twenty-Eight

Within a few days, Amos was feeling better. His face had lost some of its puffiness while the bruises had softened from vivid purple to buttercream yellow. He was using the salve the doctor had left with him when he'd come to care for Clyde. Now he could bend his fingers partway without cringing as much.

Our relationship had changed since Tom and Dan had attacked our station. While Amos and I weren't exactly chummy, we no longer avoided one another. We didn't fuss as much, either. Occasionally, Amos allowed me to saddle the Pony Express horses. It was as though I'd finally proved my mettle and Amos felt he could trust me.

Clyde had changed as well. Although he was back to his old self in appearance, he'd lost his jaunty and cocky nature. Whenever he rode through Mud Springs, he didn't joke or banter with Amos and me. Instead, he was broody, sullen, rarely offering either one of us a smile or a greeting. I worried about him, wishing I could do something to bring back his good mood.

In the weeks following my mail run, I grew restless. I was bored, hankering for more than the tedious humdrum of cooking, cleaning, pitching manure, or hauling firewood. Though it had been rough and dangerous, I missed the thrill of the ride. I longed to get back in the saddle, to feel the power of Ebony beneath me. I missed the wind in my hair, the breathtaking speed, the giddiness of being one with one of the fastest creatures on earth.

Chance seemed different as well. He stuck to me like a burr, laying across the doorway when I worked in the soddy or shadowing me when I went about my chores outdoors, as though worried I might take off again.

"Yer gonna trip me up will all yer hangin' underfoot," I teased. Yet I was grateful for his devotion and constant companionship.

Bright autumn colors began to fade as cold temperatures crept into our valley. I found myself hitching up my coat collar when I went outdoors. I spent more time in the snug soddy, cooking stews to warm us up.

Most evenings, I read the newspaper to Amos while he oiled the harnesses or sharpened tools. His hand, though badly scarred, had healed sufficiently for him to resume his regular tasks. On occasion, I caught him wincing with pain which told me his hand hadn't fully healed.

"Construction of the transcontinental telegraph system scheduled to begin," I read aloud one cold, gusty night in early December. "The telegraph poles will be planted roughly along the Pony Express route...."

I stopped reading as an angry wind whooshed around the house. The soddy sighed and shuddered with each blast from the storm. I shivered, scooting closer to the stove.

"Feels like snow," Amos said, laying aside the leather straps he was repairing.

He rose stiffly then stuffed more rags into the window slits and the gaps where chilly air seeped in. Poking among the goods on the top bunk, Amos scrounged up a hank of rope, tying one end to the door.

"Whatcha doing?" I asked, watching Amos shrug into his coat.

"Settin' up a safety line," Amos said, pulling on a pair of gloves. "Gonna tie the other end to the barn so's we can find our way back 'n forth in case we git us a blizzard."

I wondered how anyone could get lost with the soddy only thirty feet or so from the barn. I shrugged it off as one of Amos' odd activities, then thought no more about it.

The next morning, I woke to the sound of a fierce wind battering the barn. Cold drafts snuck through chinks in the walls. Snuggling closer to Chance's warm body, I hoped to catch a few more minutes' sleep.

It was no use. Now awake, I couldn't warm up.

Snugging my skimpy coat around my chest, I opened the barn door. I staggered back as freezing air blew in and took my breath away. A ferocious blizzard was raging, engulfing our valley in its vast, white depths. So dense was the whirling snow that the soddy was hidden by a blur of white.

Fat snowflakes tumbled from the sky, fast and steady, rushing in as I paused in the doorway. Chance sniffed the flakes, then growled as they landed on his nose.

"What do ya think?"

Chance covered his nose with a paw, then turned away, padding off to the far side of the barn where he curled up on a pile of hay and closed his eyes.

"Coward," I quipped, fighting the force of the wind as I put my whole weight against the door to close it.

I hunted down an empty feed sack, slashing two holes in it for my eyes. I felt a bit like an outlaw about to attack a stagecoach as I pulled the sack over my head. Slipping a pair of socks over my hands as makeshift gloves, I ventured out into the storm.

As soon as I stepped outside, a sharp, icy wind slammed into me. Gasping for air, I hunched my shoulders against the fierce wind. It tugged at my hood and stung my eyes.

I took a few steps, at once sucked into the blinding storm. For a second, I was overcome with panic. I was alone out here, just me against this solid wall of white. If, for some reason, I headed in the wrong direction....

Stop that, I chided myself, thankful for the safety line Amos had strung the previous night.

Clinging tightly to the rope, I plowed through the swirling snow. Foolishly, I glanced back, startled to notice the stable was no longer visible. A weight lodged in the pit of my stomach as I considered the fresh danger Amos and I now faced. No weapons, resources, or sheer determination could save us if we wandered in the wrong direction.

The snow was so deep each footstep was a grueling struggle. More than once, I tripped, nearly tumbling face first in the snow, but my grip on the rope kept me from falling. After what seemed like an unusually long time, I reached the soddy. The only way I knew this was because I'd run out of rope. The building was nothing more than a white mound, the door buried beneath a snow drift.

Numb with cold, I dug as fast as my little hands were able. Snow crept up my sleeves, whipped into my eyes, blew in under my coat. Even my eyelashes were stiff with frost.

When I couldn't feel my hands anymore, I gave up and turned around to head back to the barn. My footprints were no longer visible. They had already disappeared under a fresh blanket of snow.

"Amos! I yelled, fighting tears. "Amos!"

No one answered. The wind howled louder than I could yell.

Amos would never hear me out here. I was on my own.

Chapter Twenty-Nine

"One more time," I whispered, plunging my bare hands into the cold, wet snow. Suddenly, a brown piece of wood emerged amidst all the white.

"I made it!" I squealed, digging faster now.

Clearing just enough snow to squeeze through, I slid down into the tight space between the snow drift and the door. I pushed against the door. It wouldn't budge. A coat of ice had sealed the door shut.

Unnnhhh! I yelled, cold, frightened, and at my wit's end. Tears spilled over, trickling down my cheeks. Before I could wipe them away, the tears froze, tugging on my tender windburned skin.

Unnnhhh! I yelled again, fear turning into anger. With a surge of wild, reckless fury, I slammed my back against the door. It flew open with a *whack*. I tumbled headlong into the room, landing hard on the dirt floor.

"You okay?" Amos said, his mouth hanging wide open in surprise.

"Never better," I grumbled, pushing to my feet.

Lurching across the room, I held my numbed hands over the warm stove, cringing as the heat brought feeling back to my fingers. It felt like a wolf was tearing at my flesh, inch by agonizing inch.

"What's that thing on yer head?" Amos asked, squinting in the dim light of a candle.

"What, d... d... does it look like?" It was hard to speak with my teeth chattering, and my lips frozen stiff.

Dropping onto a crate, I kicked off my sock-gloves, boots, hat, and coat, scattering snow across the floor. My feet were as numb as my hands.

"Hard to tell," Amos said, lips twitching.

"Are you laughing at me?" I spoke.

Amos rose to stoke the fire. "Where's yer hat and gloves?"

"Ain't got none," I snapped. "What's with all the questions?"

"Cause I worr...," Amos began, then stopped. "'cause I don't want ya getting' sick and leavin' me with all the chores."

He picked up one of my discarded boots and turned it over. "Land sakes, boy! Ya ain't gonna survive out here, goin' 'round with holes in yer boots."

Mumbling to himself, Amos sat down in front of the fire, reached into his sewing box, and pulled out two scraps of leather. "It's a wonder ya haven't caught yer death of a cold 'fore now. Why didn't ya git yerself some new boots?"

"How 'm I gonna do that when I'm stuck in the middle of nowhere? It's not like I can jus' run into town to git me a new pair."

"Ya write down what ya need then give it to Miller or Clyde," Amos said, cutting out two leather soles. "Mr. Hammond will pick it up from the general store then bring it next time he comes this way. Mr. Slade takes the cost outta yer wages."

"Well, now. Think ya could 'a told me that sooner?"

Ignoring my remark, Amos poured hot wax into my boots then slipped in the two soles. He pressed them down with his fist until the leather insoles stuck. "Yer feet will still git a bit wet but at least it's better than holes."

While I finished thawing, Amos ventured out to feed the horses. Once I was able to bend my fingers, I set a pot of beans to simmer on the stove then cooked up some Johnnycakes. Once the cakes were ready, I began to pace, worried that Amos hadn't come back yet. What was taking him so long?

Amos finally returned, a burst of icy air blasting in behind him. I breathed a sigh of relief, surprising myself. Since when had I cared so much about this man?

"Gonna be a bad winter," Amos mumbled, stomping his feet.

I barely recognized him under the layers of snow. Yanking off his hat, coat, and gloves, he shook the snow onto the floor. Tiny mud puddles formed where the snow had landed. "Yer gonna need some mitts and a scarf or ya won't make it."

After breakfast, we gathered scraps of leather, old clothes, along with torn seed bags which we spread out on the table. I placed my hands on two scraps of leather, then Amos traced around them.

He cut two pieces for each hand allowing a one-inch seam all around for the stitching. Then, he threaded his heavy-duty needle, sewing the pieces together to make a pair of mitts.

"Not as fancy as our new President Lincoln's I warrant, but warm enough," he said, handing me my first pair of gloves.

"They fit perfectly," I said, slipping my hands into the mitts, a large grin on my face as I flexed my fingers.

"Good. Now cut several strips of cloth 'bout ten inches wide. We'll sew the ends together to make a scarf."

We worked well together. I cut the cloth and Amos sewed. Soon, I was the proud owner of a warm scarf.

I wrapped it around my neck and grinned. "Bit itchy, but it'll keep the snow from going down my neck."

"Don't need a hat," Amos said, a smile tugging at the corners of his mouth. "The one ya made is surprisingly good. Might even make one fer me so's we can rob the next stagecoach that comes through here."

Amos threw back his head and howled with laughter. This time it was honest to goodness humor instead of mockery. I laughed too. I set about clearing up the mess we'd made.

Chapter Thirty

Sometime during the night, the wind died down. But the barn stayed cold. I'd gone to sleep wearing my coat, hat, scarf, and boots. Huddling close together, Chance and I shared a buffalo robe Amos had loaned me.

By morning, the sun had come up. Delicious rays of sunlight streamed through the cracks and onto the barn floor.

"So, Chance, ya gonna go out today or jus' sleep thru it again?"

Chance thumped his tail and followed me to the door. I pulled it open, blinking at the dazzling white snow. Icicles dangled from the rooftops, glittering like shiny spangles.

Now that the snow was under foot instead of falling from above, Chance was ready to venture out. He bolted out of the barn then disappeared as he pounced, into a drift. He plowed his way out, then shook off the powdery snow, showering me in the process.

"Snow don't seem to bother him much," Amos called, tossing a shovel-full of snow over his shoulder. He was trying to clear a path from the soddy to the barn. I noticed he hadn't made much progress.

"Hang on, Amos, I'll git a shovel and dig from this end." My breath rose in a thin white cloud. I worked from the barn doors out, my boots crunching on the icy snow. "Think Miller will make it today?"

"Might be a bit late, but he'll show," Amos said. "Can't let a little snow stop the mail."

"A little snow?" I shook my head. Snow lay in deep drifts against fences and buildings. The dull, brown, muddy station had been transformed into a beautiful, dazzling white wonderland.

Amos pitched another shovelful of snow over his shoulder. "Ain't nothin' to the likes of what they've got in the mountains."

By the time Miller arrived, we had sliced a narrow path through the endless mounds of snow. All I could see of Miller were his eyes and bright red cheeks. He looked miserable despite being swathed in layers of clothing.

"Care fer some coffee to warm ya up?" I asked.

Miller shook his head. "Best keep goin'."

He tossed the Mochila onto Ebony's saddle then, with nothing more than a nod, rode away, two black specks sucked into a world of white.

* * * * *

The wintry weather stayed for several weeks, each cold, gloomy day wrapping up with an even colder night. Amos and I hunkered down tight, making the best of it by mending, cleaning, oiling, and sorting tools. We ventured out only to shovel snow, care for the horses, or saddle amount for one of the riders.

One cold wintry evening, late in December, I read unsettling news about conflicts between the northern and southern states. South Carolina had pulled out of the Union; the country was heading for war.

"Fearing an attack on Fort Moultrie," I read, "Major Anderson removes women and children to Fort Sumter just one day after Christmas…"

"Confound it!" Amos grumbled, wiping his hands on a greasy towel. "I knew I'd forget 'bout Christmas."

Slapping the rag down on the table, he pushed to his feet then stomped across the room. Kneeling on the dirt floor, he peered under his bed, muttering as he pulled out an assortment of boxes.

"Whatcha lookin' for?" I asked, intrigued by this odd behavior.

Amos continued to root around under the bed, ignoring my question.

"Aha!" He cried, emerging with a big sack marked *beans* which he dumped in my lap.

"What's this?"

"Supposed to be yer Christmas present," Amos mumbled. "But I plum missed the day."

Christmas present? From Amos? Somehow, I couldn't wrap my head around this.

"Ya gonna open it or jus' sit there gawkin' all day?"

Reaching into the sack, I felt something soft touch my skin. Slowly, I pulled out a beautiful buckskin coat. Gently, I ran a hand gently across the soft coat, unable to speak for the knot that had formed in my throat.

"Try it on," Amos said, grinning.

I slipped the coat on, snugging it against my chest. The coat was a tad big but I didn't care. Besides, it would give me room to grow.

Impulsively, I threw my arms around Amos. Amos wasn't quite sure how to respond. Instead of hugging me back, he patted me on the shoulder, then quickly pulled away.

"Right. Well, time's a wastin'. Got chores to do."

I watched Amos as he bundled up against the cold, then slipped out.

"Ain't ever gonna figure ya out, ya ol' coot," I told the empty room, my voice cracking with emotion. "Jus' when I think I can't stand ya no more, ya go and do somethin' like this."

Chapter Thirty-One

I wore that buckskin coat all winter long. It was a bit cumbersome since it was a couple sizes too large, but it did it keep me warm outdoors as I went about my chores. The coat also kept me snug during the long, frigid nights.

Amos and I didn't bicker as much now. I understood his gift was not just meant to keep me from getting sick, although Amos would stick to that theory all the way to his death bed. The coat was his way of showing he'd accepted me.

Eventually the sun came out, strong and bright, melting the snow. The buildings began to emerge from their snowy cocoons while shallow brown rivulets trickled across the yard, turning white snow into dirty, slushy, muddy puddles.

Birds trilled their greetings. Crickets chirped once more. Brilliant yellow flowers popped up overnight to smarten up our soddy's loamy roof. Sparrows and cardinals fluttered down from the cottonwoods, splashing gleefully in the muddy pools.

One delightful morning, a pair of goldfinches were all atwitter, arguing over a small puddle. I hovered in the doorway of the barn, listening to their chatter until Chance dashed past and chased them away.

As soon as the route was passable, Mr. Hammond arrived with fresh goods to restock our dwindling supplies. He brought fatty bacon, potatoes, flour, coffee, sugar, molasses, salt, cornmeal, and Amos' favorite; pickles cured in brine. Each time, he left a copy of the *St. Joseph Gazette*. The news was unsettling as the war between north and south began to heat up. Yet in our quiet little corner of the world, the war seemed very distant.

Now the weather had warmed up, we went back to patching the soddy. Mice had burrowed deep into the walls during the winter, leaving holes in all four sides of the house. The roof, leaky as ever, had to be completely replaced just like the previous spring.

Several times, we had to pause in our work as a massive swoop of sandhill cranes soared across the valley, their tightly packed formation obscuring the sun. They were migrating back to the sandhills just north of us. Their raucous bugle calls echoed for miles, deafening and harsh.

By June, the days had already turned lazy-hot and sticky. Not even a breeze wafted through the sluggish valley. Most days, I used the excuse I was hauling water to take a quick dip in the springs. Mosquitos were everywhere this year, eager for fresh blood. I couldn't sleep under the willow tree for fear of being bitten head to toe.

One morning, I woke up feeling poorly. I sat up then fell back on the straw as a blinding headache crippled me. My arms ached; my legs felt leaden. I was sweating but shrugged it off as muggy weather. Groaning from the effort, I pushed myself into a sitting position, my back against a wall, my head feeling like it was about to burst.

"Let's go to the springs," I said to Chance. Despite the voracious mosquitos, I wanted to get out of the broiling heat. "Maybe it'll help my head."

Stumbling like a drunken man, I edged my way down to the springs, squinting against the sun's glare.

I'll just take a dip, I thought. *Just a quick dip to cool down.*

Chance didn't hesitate but jumped right in. Too tired to take another step, I collapsed on the buffalo grass. Eyes closed, I listened to the leaves rustling overhead. They sounded like voices, whispering back and forth.

Chance knew something was wrong, leaving the springs to come check on me. He began to whine, nudging me gently with his wet nose.

"Ain't... feelin'... good," I stammered, reaching out with my eyes shut tightly against the sun.

Curled up beside me, Chance continued to whine. I stroked the dog's wet fur, waiting for the pain beating in my temples to go away. Wave upon wave of dizziness and nausea washed over me.

Shivering uncontrollably, I squinted up at the sky, wondering if a storm was blowing in. All I saw were white horses flying across the blue heavens.

"Chance! Look! Flyin' horses! We gotta tell Amos about this!"

As I struggled to rise, my wobbly legs buckled under me. I crumpled like a sack of potatoes, my head hitting the ground with a sickening thud--silence and absolute darkness.

* * * * *

Someone was trying to wake me. Rough hands touched my face, gripped my arms.

Blindly, I struck out. "Billy... Billy," a muffled voice called over and over. The voice was loud, insistent, tugging me from the sleep I craved. Why wouldn't he stop and leave me be?

"Billy... Billy." The voice grew fainter.

I tried to open my eyes, but they seemed to be swollen shut. Suddenly, I felt something firm and strong wrap around my body, then lift me off the ground. It squeezed me tightly, smothering me.

"Let me go!" I screamed, kicking and thrashing. I struggled to fight off the evil snake coiling tighter around me.

"Billy...," the voice called again.

For just a moment, my vision cleared, enough for me to look up into the face of the one holding me.

Amos.

"Hush, now," he said softly.

Comforted, I laid my head against Amos' chest then fell asleep.

Chapter Thirty-Two

When I woke up, I discovered Amos had tucked me in bed with a cool, wet cloth across my forehead.

"Drink this," Amos said, lifting my head. I cried out as pain shot through my head.

"Drink," Amos insisted, pressing a cup to my lips.

I tried to take a sip, but my lips wouldn't obey. Water dribbled down my chin.

"Try agin'," Amos coaxed.

This time a few drops made it past my dry lips but didn't take away the bitter taste in my mouth.

"Git some sleep," Amos said as he lowered my head back onto the pillow.

At last, I stopped struggling and drifted off to sleep.

* * * * *

Bitter drinks. Frightful dreams. Restless sleep. Whispers. Doors opening and closing. Soft footsteps. Cool cloths. Dim faces. Pain. Voices.

It was all I knew.

Then, nothing.

* * * * *

Slowly the world came back into focus. I struggled to sit up, but a heavy weight pushed against my chest, holding me down. I inched one hand across the blanket, surprised to discover a mass of soft, warm fur was laying on top of me. For a second, I thought it must be Chance but that couldn't be right. Amos refused to let him come inside the soddy. But it was Chance.

"Chance?" I mumbled through dry, swollen lips.

Chance sidled closer, licking my flushed face as his tail thumped against my leg.

"Thought ya might like some company," a deep voice said.

Slowly, I turned my head, wincing from the pain. Amos's blurry face floated in and out of my vision.

Sliding a large hand under my head, Amos lifted it slightly off the pillow. "Drink this," he said, pressing a cup to my mouth.

My teeth rattled against the tin cup. I grimaced as the water touched my swollen lips, but I sipped it anyway, soothed as the cool, refreshing water trickled over my tongue and down my sore throat.

"Had me worried, ya little scamp," Amos said, gentling easing my head back down.

"What's... wrong?" I whispered.

"Doc says it's malaria. Now stop talkin' and git some rest." Amos tucked the cover around my shoulders.

I closed my eyes against the thundering pain in my head.

Amos took my hand and squeezed it gently.

"Don't ever scare me like that agin'," I heard him say, as I drifted off to sleep.

Chapter Thirty-Three

I slept most of the time, waking only when Amos brought me some water or a thin broth to drink. As I grew more aware of my surroundings, I tried to sit up. At first my head felt heavy, wobbly as a baby's.

The movement made my head swim. My stomach churned as the room dipped and swayed crazily to the left, then to the right. Closing my eyes, I gently eased myself back down, repeating the exercise till I could sit up without feeling so woozy.

"What ya need is some sun and fresh air," Amos said one morning, yanking off the blanket. "Come on, let's git ya outta bed."

With one arm around my waist, Amos helped me stand. My legs were flimsy as a scarecrow's. If Amos hadn't been holding me, I would have dropped to the floor.

"Reckon yer gonna need a little more help." Amos scooped me up as easily as a sack of flour, then carried me outside. He settled me on the ground, propped against the soddy wall.

It wasn't comfortable but the warm sun on my face felt wonderful after all that time in bed. The cool breeze blowing through the valley felt fresh and clean and helped clear away some of the cobwebs in my muddled brain.

Chance was delighted to have me outdoors again, dashing wildly to the edge of the yard then back. He seemed a bit confused, barking. Running a few paces. Running back to me as if to say. "Come on, play with me."

"Sorry, buddy," I said, stroking the dog's head. "I ain't good fer much right now."

Chance finally gave up and laid down beside me, his head in my lap. We nodded off, sleeping until Amos nudged me awake.

"Let's git ya back to bed before ya topple over."

Gathering me in his arms, he carried me back to bed then snugged the covers around me. I quickly fell into a healing sleep.

* * * * *

Once I was strong enough to totter around on my own, I tried doing some of my easier chores. I tired quickly and didn't have half the strength I used to. I often woke up feeling as tired as when I'd gone to bed. Tasks I'd once taken for granted now wore me out.

Amos hovered like a mother hen. "Ain't gonna do me no good if ya wear yerself out. Jus' gonna git sick again," he'd grumble.

Then one evening, while Amos and I were sitting outside watching the sun set over the western hills, I decided it was time to ask about my illness.

"The last thing I remember is feeling sick. What happened?"

"Yer friend here came to find me, barkin' like a crazed animal. Knew somethin' was wrong so I followed him. He led me down to the springs. Can't tell ya how sick I was, thinkin' ya might 'a drowned. Then I saw ya, lyin' under a tree, ramblin' on and on 'bout flyin' horses and other nonsense."

His voice cracked.

"Carried ya home, kickin' and punchin', fightin' against me like some wild animal. Soon as Miller arrived, I told him we needed a doc real quick. When the doc got here, he took one look at ya and said it was malaria. Fixed ya up with some medicine called quinine."

"Malaria?"

"It's a sickness ya sometimes get from mosquito bites." His voice held a tremor. "Doc said if ya wasn't so young 'n strong, ya probably wouldn't 'a made it."

For a moment silence hung heavily in the air. In the east, an explosion of color tinted the sky a beautiful shade of crimson.

Amos cleared his throat. When he spoke, his voice sounded strained. "When I was about yer age, I had a brother named Adam. When we wasn't bickerin', we was good friends, goin' fishin', swimmin', and hikin' together."

Amos gave a bitter laugh. "One day I woke up sneezin' and feelin' poorly. Adam and I was gonna go swimmin' in the creek that day but Ma sent me back to bed, tellin' Adam to let me sleep. Adam knew Pa didn't want us kids to go down to the creek alone. But Adam was a stubborn boy. He could git into a peck 'a trouble real fast. That night when Adam didn't git home fer supper...."

Amos stopped, staring out at the horizon for several minutes. Tears began to trickle down his cheeks.

I could guess what was coming next. I didn't want to hear it. I didn't want to hear the raw pain in Amos' voice.

"Ya don't have to continue....," I started.

Amos shook his head then picked up where he'd left off.

"I told Pa 'bout Adam wantin' to go swimmin' so Pa took a lantern and went lookin' fer him, shoutin' and callin' till he was hoarse. Found Adam next day... washed ashore... down river... dead."

I shuddered as Amos uttered this last word.

"I'm sorry," I whispered.

Amos shrugged then pushed to his feet. He looked so sad with his lips pressed tightly together, his shoulders sagging. "So, when yer dog fetched me and headed to the springs, it brought it all back. Thought ya might have...." He didn't finish, just turned then shuffled slowly away.

I retreated to my nest in the barn, knowing Amos needed time alone. I lay awake for a while, thinking about the terrible story I'd just heard. When I finally fell asleep, I dreamed I was struggling to swim across Rush Creek.

I cried and called for help, but no one answered. I fought the powerful current sweeping me further and further downstream till it finally sucked me under... deep into a brown watery grave.

Chapter Thirty-Four

My lengthy illness, along with Amos' dreadful tale, helped heal our relationship. We talked more, squabbled less, and worked well together.

But despite the progress, I was growing more and more restless. When I looked to the hills circling the station, I felt trapped, like a bucket down a well. Amos must have sensed it for he started teaching me how to shoe a horse, repair a harness, sew leather, and mend fences.

Then, one warm July morning, my life changed. I had just cleaned up the breakfast dishes and was on my way to the stables to muck out the stalls when Miller rode into the station.

"Got something for you, Billy," he said, sliding off the horse.

"Me?" I was shocked.

Miller nodded as he unlocked one of the Mochila's pockets. His hand dove into the pouch, then pulled out a letter wrapped in oil cloth. "It's from…," he paused dramatically, grinning at me.

My heart pounded with a mingle of excitement and worry. "Go on," I said, thumping Miller's arm.

"It's from a Mr.... Joseph... Sade.... Spade... oh, Slade! Know anyone by that name?"

"Jus' give it to me, will ya?" I laughed, snatching the letter.

With a chuckle, Miller shifted the Mochila onto Aurora's back, swung into the saddle, then flicked the reins.

"Happy reading!" he yelled as he shot out of the station.

For a few moments I was speechless, staring at my name scrawled across the envelope in large letters. When I looked up, I noticed Amos standing in the doorway, watching me.

"Come on, Thunder." I pocketed the letter then led the horse to be curried.

The poor animal was in a lather. I removed the bridle and saddle, then briskly rubbed him down, my hands working rhythmically as I mulled over the contents of the letter. Once Thunder's breathing had eased, I gave in, fishing the letter from my pocket. It was so crinkled, I had to smooth it out.

July 18, 1861
Mr. Billy Barber,
On behalf of Misters Russell, Majors and Waddell, I wish to express my sincerest appreciation for your loyal service to the Central Overland California and Pike's Peak Express Company.

The encouraging reports we receive from Mr. Perkins combined with your commendable assistance in relaying the mail to Scott's Bluff last fall have brought you to our attention.

We currently have a rider position available and would like to extend the offer to you.
I eagerly await your favorable reply.
Mr. Joseph Slade, Superintendent.

"I did it, Chance, I did it!" I shouted, punching the air with my fist. "I'm gonna be a Pony Express rider!"

With no idea why I was so thrilled, but happy nonetheless, Chance barked loudly, wagging his tail as he ran in circles around me.

"They want *me*, Chance. *Me!*"

I spun around in circles, Chance watching me curiously. I twirled around once more, suddenly finding myself face to face with Amos. I felt the heat in my face and dropped my gaze.

"Jus' spotted the supply wagon comin' down the hill," Amos said curtly, then turned and walked away.

"He heard me, didn't he?" I said, glancing down at Chance.

The dog barked and thumped his tail.

"Thought so too."

Leading Thunder to the corral, I released him, then plodded out to the yard. Amos had already started unloading the supplies.

"Hey, Billy!" Mr. Hammond called out, waving to me.

"Howdy, Mr. Hammond." I waved back. "Got some good stuff fer us?"

"Maybe." He chuckled.

Lifting down a box marked *Mud Springs,* I carried it into the soddy, avoiding Amos' gaze as we passed.

Anxious to avoid him, I started unpacking the crates instead of helping unload the last few sacks. I heard the wagon leave. Several minutes later, Amos wandered in with a sack. He dumped it on the floor then sat down on a crate, watching me work.

Opening one of the new crates, I pulled out several jars of molasses and honey, stacking them on the top bunk. I could feel Amos' eyes on my back. A heavy silence filled the room as I opened the next crate and pulled out a sack of flour.

I couldn't stand the tension any longer.

"Dern it, Amos!" I exploded. "Ya gonna sit there all day or help?"

In my anger, I banged the bag of flour on the table. It burst open, sending a powdery cloud of flour flying into the air. I regretted the outburst as soon as it happened, bracing for a sharp scolding.

Instead, I heard a chuckle.

I glanced at Amos. He looked so funny with creamy-white powder in his hair. I had a hunch I looked the same. I sputtered, then broke into a fit of laughter. Our eyes met and all the tension that had built up between us dissolved as we burst into a fit of laughter.

Chapter Thirty-Five

"Slade wants ya to ride, don't he?" Amos said. I nodded.

"I'll be mighty sorry to lose ya....," Amos stopped then cleared the tremor from his throat. "But that's not what matters. I'm happy fer ya if that's what ya wanna do."

He slapped his thighs, then stood. "Better git back to work. Dern wind's gonna blow the fence down afore I can fix it."

With a noticeable sag to his shoulders, Amos ducked out the door. I cleared the table, feeling like I'd failed him even though I hadn't done anything wrong.

"It's my life!" I griped, tossing dirty plates into the dishpan. "And I ain't gonna waste it scooping poop!"

Snatching up the dishrag, I started scrubbing the dishes with a vigorous swipe of the hand. I scrubbed so fast and so hard, water spilled over, trickling across the table and onto the floor, forming a muddy puddle.

Once the dishes were done, I carried the dishpan outside to dump the dirty water behind the soddy. A familiar coyote yell and the *thump, thump,*

thump of horse's hooves sent me rushing back around to the front.

A lone rider was slowly coming down the eastern hill. He was too far for me to see his face clearly, but I recognized the rider's thick crop of copper curls. Clyde? How could it be? Miller had just come through with the mail.

Clyde rode in on a grey mare, looking smart in a new coat, buckskin pants, and shiny leather boots. Wisps of hair curled around his boyish face. His runaway freckles danced like sparks of firelight and his sassy grin lit up his face.

"Hey kid," he yelled, beaming. "Got a few crumbs to spare for an old, wounded rider just passin' through?"

Chance dashed up to him, wagging his tail as though he hadn't seen Clyde for years. Clyde reached down and patted him on the head.

"Whatcha doin' on that ol' thing?" I asked, staring at the skinny horse.

"I'm headin' to Ca-li-for-nia," he crowed, his voice filled with excitement. "Gonna find me some gold!"

"What about the Pony Express?" I asked, wondering if the hot sun had scrambled his brains.

"I quit."

Stunned, I dropped the dishpan, then stared dumbly at the rivulet of soapy water trickling across the yard.

"Whatcha doin' with that ol' thing?" Amos asked, strolling out of the barn.

"Just cause she ain't pullin' at the bit don't mean she's no good," said Clyde. "Got her at a fair price."

Amos' eyebrows shot up. "What's wrong with 'er?"

"Ain't nothin' wrong with her!" Clyde argued, throwing up his hands in despair.

"What about yer job?" Amos asked.

Clyde shook his head. "Gosh, you two are something else, asking the same dumb questions."

I glanced at Amos and shrugged. "He quit."

"That's right. I'm headed to Ca-li-for-nia to pan for gold. Got sick and tired of all the dangers, much less listenin' to Slade naggin' me about my unfinished ride to Scott's Bluff." …." His voice grew lower like Mr. Slade's. "I've been shot several times and no bullet wound ever stopped me."

"Yer kiddin'," I said. But the sour look on Clyde's face suggested he was telling the truth.

"Some people don't care 'bout others, so long as they git what they want. That's Slade. Shuffles people like a deck of cards." A hint of bitterness had crept into his voice.

I thought back to the day when Slade had offered… no, informed me… I was going to Mud Springs. Could it be Clyde was right about Mr. Slade? I wondered about the crumpled letter in my pocket. Did Slade want me as a replacement for Clyde? The thought was unsettling. I shifted uncomfortably from one foot to the other and kept quiet about the letter.

"Ya realize pannin' fer gold is hard work, don't ya?" Amos asked. "No guarantees either."

"I know." Clyde shrugged.

"Go on in then," Amos said, waving a hand towards the soddy. "Git yerself somethin' to eat before ya head out again. I'll git yer pony a drink."

"She's *not* a pony," Clyde muttered.

Amos led the mare towards the drinking trough. "Whatever."

Grinning, Clyde followed me across the yard. "Can't stay long. Wanna get to Scott's Bluff before the storm hits."

I glanced up at the clear blue sky. "Storm?"

"Sure," Clyde said, sniffing the air. "Can't you smell it?"

I lifted my nose and sniffed. Chance let loose a sharp bark.

"Billy doing it wrong?" Clyde chuckled, patting the dog's head.

Chance stopped at the doorway, then sat down and waited while Clyde and I ducked into the soddy. I lifted the coffee pot off the fire and poured my friend a cup of coffee.

"Sorry I don't have any Johnnycakes, but I wasn't expectin' ya."

"That's okay." Clyde blew on the steaming liquid then took a sip. He squeezed his eyes shut. "Hoo-boy! Amos' coffee is bitter enough to curl the hairs on a dead man."

Clyde puckered his lips. "Think I'll pass on the coffee. Got some switchel instead?" he asked, setting the cup on the table.

"Just made a fresh batch of ginger-water this morning," I said, fetching him a glass.

He drained it in one go.

I laughed as he set the glass on the table. "I'm gonna miss ya, Clyde."

"I'm gonna miss you too," Clyde said, tousling my hair. He slid a hand into his pocket then pulled out a used deck of cards. He thrust them into my hand.

"Take these. It'll give you and Amos somethin' fun to do fer a change."

My heart sank. I couldn't tell him I wouldn't be here much longer. "Thank you," I said, instead.

We sauntered out to where Amos waited with Clyde's horse.

"Best be off," Clyde said. "My mare's a good horse but slow as molasses. Probably be an old man by the time we get to California."

Then Clyde opened a pocket on the saddle and pulled out a bottle of brandy. He handed it to Amos. The usual gleam of mischief shone in his eyes. "Fer medicinal purposes," he whispered behind one hand.

He turned, winked at me, then mounted his mare.

"Wa-hoo!" he yelled. "Ca-li-for-nia, here I come!"

With a shriek, Clyde sank his spurs into the horse's flanks. The startled mare whinnied then slowly trotted off. Amos and I watched him crest the western hill, whooping and hollering as he went.

"Them Californians are in fer a real treat," Amos said, shaking his head. He scowled at the bottle in his hands, but under the frown was a faint trace of amusement. "Not sure if I envy 'em or pity 'em."

Chapter Thirty-Six

That night, I couldn't sleep. I tossed and turned, wavering between two options. Should I go or should I stay? What once would have been an easy choice now filled me with worry.

Confused thoughts and snippets of conversations buzzed through my brain like a swarm of bees; ... *sick and tired of riskin' my life... Some people don't care 'bout others, so long as they git what they want...It's my life... I'll be sorry to lose ya....*

Thunder growled somewhere in the distance, a welcome distraction to all this brooding.

"So, Clyde was right about the storm after all," I told Chance. "Come on, let's go watch."

Ever since I had come to Mud Springs, I had been fascinated by the fierce thunderstorms which rolled into the valley. I loved to stand outside as I watched its stealthy approach. Chance, on the other hand, hated the storms. Reluctantly, he followed me outside, huddling in fear between my legs.

The sky was pitch black without a star in sight. Lightning flashed every few seconds, quickly followed by crashing thunder.

Zap! flashed the lightening.

Boom! answered the thunder.

I was so captivated by the beauty of the storm; I didn't notice Amos until he handed me a piping hot cup.

"Thought I might find ya out here," he said.

I held up a hand. "No thanks, Amos. I don't care fer any."

"It's tea," Amos said.

I took the mug, sniffed the hot liquid, then took a small, cautious sip.

"Pretty good!" I said, surprised.

"Used to make tea fer Ma," Amos said, softly. "Put tea down on my last supply order. Thought you'd like it instead of coffee."

I was touched he'd thought of me. I took another sip, watching the sky thrash and flail about. But my mind was not really on the storm.

"Ya don't want me to go, do ya?" I blurted out.

"Bah, we can manage," Amos mumbled, slurping his coffee.

"Oh."

It was definitely not the answer I'd been expecting. I blinked in surprise.

A bolt of lightning ripped through the black sky, followed closely by a bellow of thunder. Chance whimpered, leaning heavily against my right leg. I reached down and patted him on the head.

"It's just... well, I've wanted to be a Pony Express rider fer so long..."

Amos didn't say anything. I paused, mesmerized as the sky lit up with a powerful spear of lightning.

Thunder growled from the heavens like some big, terrible ogre. Chance whimpered.

"... life here is so... so... unexcitin'... it's borin'," I finished.

"Nothin' wrong with borin'," Amos replied.

A deafening crash of thunder made me jump. Terrified, Chance cowered, whining pitifully.

"Come here, Chance," Amos called, crouching down to the dog's level.

Startled, I watched as Chance darted over to him then buried his face in Amos' cupped hands. Amos spoke softly to the dog, petting him all the while. To my surprise, Chance stopped whining. I felt snubbed. When had these two become so chummy? Was it during my ride to Scott's Bluff or during my illness? Or both?

A sickening thought struck me. What would I do with Chance? I couldn't take him along on the mail rides. But I couldn't leave him behind either, even with someone like Amos. Chance was my dog. The realization filled me with anguish.

I swiped impatiently at the tears welling in my eyes. "I jus' don't wanna be a measly station attendant fer the rest of my life. I wanna prove I can do bigger things."

"Ya don't need to prove nothin', Billy," Amos replied, his voice gentler than I had ever heard it. "Ya've already done that."

Unable to hold them back any longer, I let the tears come. As if in sympathy, the clouds opened, releasing a torrent of rain.

"Better git back inside, 'fore we both catch cold," Amos mumbled.

He ducked back into the soddy while I wandered back to the barn where I shed my wet clothing, tossing it distractedly over a stall door. I lay down, Chance flopping down beside me. I snuggled close to the dog's warm, comforting body, burying my face in his soft fur.

I was like a caged animal whose door has finally been opened, uncertain whether to stay in the security of my cage or run free. Because freedom usually includes a degree of loss.

"I can't leave ya," I said, crying into Chance's neck.

Chance licked my face, his breath heavy with the scent of salty meat.

Instantly, I stopped crying. My eyes snapped open. I pulled away. "What's that smell on yer breath?" It smelled like... like... Suddenly, it all came clear. I knew why Chance had left my side to run into Amos' arms.

"Amos, you sneak!" I laughed.

Here I thought Amos had bonded with Chance while all along he'd been feeding him jerky!

Chapter Thirty-Seven

The next day, during the noonday heat, Amos and I retreated to the soddy so I could read the *St. Joseph Gazette* aloud to Amos while he sharpened his axe blade. Even though last night's thunderstorm had quickly passed, the storm in my mind continued to brew. I had postponed making any decision about the job offer till I'd had more time to think. Slade's letter lay crumpled in my coat pocket; I'd read and reread it several times.

The newspaper did nothing to improve my mood, its pages brimming with chilling news about the war.

"I seem to recall when this darn war started, no one thought it would last more'n a few weeks," Amos grumbled as he ran his thumb against the blade to check its sharpness. He scowled and picked up his whetstone again.

"Another victory for the Confederate army," I read, trying to drown out the grating sound of metal against stone. "The Union has suffered another defeat at Manassas Junction…"

My eyes were drawn to the opposite page where a list of soldiers deceased in battle ran top to bottom.

One name stood out from the rest: Raymond Daniel Greenfield.

My eyes widened in surprise and my mind scrambled to grasp what I had just read. Although it was possible another man had the same name, deep down, I knew; it was my pa.

The paper slid out of my hands and fell to the ground.

Amos looked up. "What's the matter?"

"No... nothing," I said, rushing to the door.

Standing in the yard, I fought warring emotions. I'd thought I hated my pa, wanted nothing more to do with him. Yet now he'd died, fighting in a war that was ripping our country apart, I felt oddly sad. The impact of this news suddenly hit me. I was truly an orphan now. It was no longer wishful thinking, but reality.

Part of me wanted to tell Amos the truth. Hadn't he proved he cared about me, at least a little? Another part of me wanted to hold on to my secret just a while longer. I did my best to avoid Amos the rest of that day even though I could tell he was worried about me. I knew he wanted answers, yet for some reason, I just couldn't bring myself to tell him the truth.

That evening, as I walked into the soddy, I saw Amos getting ready to toss the newspaper into the stove. He was using it as kindling so he could revive the flames and fix himself a pot of coffee.

"No!" I yelled, dashing across the room. He stared at me in shock as I snatched the paper out of his hand. "Don't use this."

"What.... What's up, Billy? Why are ya acting so strange today?"

"My... my...," I paused.

Snatching a pot resting on the stove, I mumbled something about fetching water to cook supper, then fled outdoors. Clouds, dark as my thoughts, were rolling in. Slowly, I paced back and forth to give myself time to think. Should I tell Amos the truth? I thought of all the consequences that might result. Yet, though not exactly fond of each other, Amos and I had reached a place of trust and mutual respect.

"My pa's name is in the paper," I said, bursting into the soddy. The words tumbled from my mouth. "He's on the list of soldiers killed in the war."

There. I'd told him. In a way, I was relieved. I wouldn't have to live a lie anymore.

Amos wiped his hands on a rag and sat down. "I thought you was an orphan?"

"I... I ran away from home," I said, sitting across from him.

It was surprising how much better I felt telling him the truth. I told him about my pa's abuse, my escape, the change of name....

"And yer ma?" Amos asked, his voice softer.

"She died the day I was born."

"So, I'm guessing ya ain't really Billy Barber?"

"Nah. I just used that name so Pa couldn't track me down. Name's really William Theodore Greenfield."

Amos' eyes widened and his mouth dropped open. He was staring at me as though I'd grown a second head.

"What was... yer... yer ma's name?" He twisted the cleaning rag in his hands like he was strangling a chicken for dinner.

"Theodora."

Amos' face turned a shade of grey unlike anything I had ever seen before. His voice had turned so quiet, I could barely hear him. "And her birth name?"

"Don't reckon I ever knew," I said. "But I've got her Bible. There's a whole lot of names written on the first page. Ya know, births, marriages, deaths."

"Go git it," Amos said, his voice quivering.

Confused, yet somehow knowing this was important, I ran to the barn. I retrieved my mother's Bible from my bag then hurried back to the soddy. I laid the Bible on the table, then opened it to the cover page. I ran a finger down the listings until I found the record of my parents' marriage.

I read it aloud. "Theodora Emily Perkins and Raymond Daniel Greenfield, united in marriage, June 20, 1847."

I glanced up, startled to hear Amos' strangled sob. For a moment he just stared at me, then he stood up and took a step towards me. The look in his eyes frightened me.

"I shoulda known, I shoulda known," Amos kept repeating, shaking his head as he gently grabbed my shoulders, holding me out at arms' length. "Ya got yer ma's green eyes and the same smile."

"Ya knew... Ya knew my... ma?" I choked on the last word.

"Sure did," Amos whispered, as he wrapped me in a crushing hug. "She was my little sister."

Chapter Thirty-Eight

With just one word, my world changed.
"What?" I croaked, pushing out of Amos' embrace. My throat felt so tight I could hardly speak.

Amos' laughter mingled with great big tears of joy. "Yer ma was my little sister."

I gulped.

"So, you're my…my… uncle?" The word felt so unfamiliar and strange on my tongue.

"Reckon so."

For a while, neither one of us spoke, too shocked for words. My mind ran through a range of emotions. I didn't know whether to laugh or cry. I did both, laughing through misty eyes. I was no longer an orphan. I was part of a family, be it even just one person.

Amos' laughter mingled with mine. It was a shared laughter, a healing laughter, a bridge connecting two lonely, hurting people.

At last, I found my voice. "How come Pa never told me 'bout ya?"

"Don't think yer pa wanted to."

"Why's that?"

Amos cleared his throat. "When Adam died, our family fell apart. Ma cried a lot and Pa grew moody. He hardly ever talked anymore. So, Theo - that's what I used to call yer ma - and I found jobs in town, workin' after school and on weekends so's we could keep away from home. I worked on a friend's farm and Theo did some sewin' fer a tailor.'

"Then one day, Theo came home all excited, told Ma and Pa she was in love. Pa wasn't happy. Asked her the guy's name."

"Raymond Greenfield, she'd said. Told pa they wanted to git married."

Amos paused and shook his head. "Pa was mad as a bulldog, sayin' there was no way his daughter was goin' to marry one of them good-fer-nothin' Greenfield boys. Called 'em a pack 'a no-good, whiskey-lovin' drunks."

"I'm agreed with yer pa 'bout that," I said.

"Reckon so. But Theo wouldn't listen. She ran off with the guy. Sent us a letter a few days later sayin' they got married. Pa was so stompin' mad, he wrote back. Told her she wasn't welcome in our home anymore. Near broke my heart. Ma's too." His remark came out sounding bitter and angry.

I listened closely, hanging on every word.

"One day we gits a letter from Raymond, sayin' Theo had died. He gave no reason. Said nothin' 'bout havin' a son. Ma and Pa reckoned Raymond must 'a killed her in one of his drunken rages. Guess they figured wrong."

"What about yer ma and pa?" I asked. "Where are they?

"They died, 'bout three years ago. Doc' said it was the ague, but I reckon they'd lost their will to live."

A hush filled the soddy as Amos fought back tears. His voice sounded wistful. "I came to this isolated place, thinkin' I could git away from everythin' and everybody. Too many memories in that house. Out here, there was no one to worry 'bout but me and the horses. Till ya came along and wormed yer way into my life...."

Amos choked on his words. When he looked at me, his face was twisted half in sorrow, half in joy.

"... and wormed yer way into my heart."

Epilogue

"That should be it," Amos said, heaving a large crate onto the wagon. "Ready to go?"

From my seat astride Ebony, I glanced around, taking a last good look at Mud Springs station.

So, this is it, I thought, as a horde of thoughts and emotions whirled through my brain. *Oddly enough, I'm going to miss this place.*

In the days following our discovery, Amos and I spent hours talking about my ma. He spoke at length about their childhood. He showed me the pictures from his box. Now these people in the photos had names.

They were family. My family. They were my family.

I wanted him to tell me everything he knew about my mother. After so many years wondering what kind of woman she was and what she looked like, I was eager to learn everything I could about her. I was thrilled to find out I was more like my ma than my pa.

I also sent a letter to Mr. Slade, declining his offer to become a mail rider. I had found something far better and had no desire to leave my new-found family.

A few months later, Amos received a letter from the firm of Russell, Majors and Waddell saying the Pony Express was closing all its stations.

"Says here, they're bankrupt," he said, scowling. "Gonna close the Pony Express."

"What?" I gasped, shocked at this sudden turn of events. "But... but they only started the Pony Express...," Billy counted silently on his fingers. "18... 19 months ago!"

"You know all them telegraph posts they've been putting up along the mail route?" Amos said. "They's gonna run telegraph lines all the way to California. No need fer speedy riders anymore."

"What's gonna become of Mud Springs?" I asked.

"They's gonna turn it into a telegraph office."

Shocked silence filled the room as Amos scratched the stubble on his chin. Then he went on.

"They's giving me the 'opportunity' to run the telegraph office, if I want it," Amos snorted.

He crumpled up the letter then tossed it across the room.

"I'd rather deal with a bunch of ornery animals any day than some newfangled contraption," he said, slapping the table with his hand. "Come on, let's go feed them horses.

I couldn't help but fret the rest of the day, wondering what was to become of me. What would I do, where would I go? Worse yet, would Amos go his own way and let me figure out what I wanted to do with my life? The possibility was so upsetting, I cried behind the barn.

Finally, I couldn't stand it anymore. I approached Amos later that afternoon as he sat, nursing a cup of coffee.

"What are ya gonna do now the station's closin'?"

"Well, I been thinkin'," Amos said, slurping his drink. "With all the money I bin savin', I reckon I got 'nough to buy me a few head of cattle. Figure it's 'bout time fer me to head on back to Fiddle Creek."

"Where's that?" I asked, too scared to even ask if Amos' plans involved me.

"That's where I used to live. Pa owned a couple hundred acres there. Good farmin' land. Pa left it all to me, but I was so broken up 'bout my entire family dyin', I left jus' to git away from all the memories."

I swallowed the knot forming in my throat, turning away so Amos wouldn't see the tears threatening to spill from my eyes. Had I found my uncle, only to lose him so soon?

"Thought ya might wanna come too," Amos said. His voice held a note of fondness. "Sure, could use an extra set of hands to help with the farm."

I whirled around. "Ya mean it? Ya really mean it?"

"Every word," Amos replied, grinning.

I raced over, throwing my arms around the big man's neck.

"Now don't git soft on me," Amos laughed. "Jus' 'cause yer family don't mean I don't expect ya to earn yer keep."

It didn't take long for us to pack our few belongings and stack them in the wagon. Now here we were, on a cold November day, closing the soddy's door for the last time.

I glanced down at Chance, then over at Aurora and Thunder who were tied to the back of the wagon. Amos had bought all three horses from Russell, Majors and Waddell so we'd have good, reliable horses for the farm.

"Everyone one ready?" he asked.

Chance wagged his tail eagerly, prepared to follow me wherever I might go. The horses whinnied and tossed their heads. Amos grinned.

"Fiddle Creek, here we come," he shouted, flicking the reins.

Slowly, we pulled out, heading up the northern hill. At the top, I turned and cast one last glance at the station below.

I'd never forget Mud Springs station.

After all, this was the place where I'd found love.

Historical Note

Mud Springs station is located in the south-central part of Morrill County, Nebraska. Overland travelers first used the springs in the 1850s. In 1860-1861, the station became a telegraph office.

On February 4-6, 1865, the Battle of Mud Springs took place. Nine soldiers stationed there, held out until reinforcements arrived and the warriors withdrew. The telegraph station was abandoned in 1877. All that remains of Mud Springs station is a marker.

It is listed in the National Register of Historic Places.

While most of the characters in this book are fictional, Mr. Joseph Alfred "Jack" Slade was, in fact, the superintendent for the Central Overland California & Pike's Peak Express Co., commonly known as the Pony Express.

He had a reputation for being a hard, ferocious, vengeful man. In his book, *Roughing It,* Mark Twain calls him a desperado, and goes on to describe a man whose hate tortured him until vengeance appeased it.

A man named James McArdle served as the station keeper.

Bibliography

Burton, Richard F, *The City of the Saints and Across the Rocky Mountains to California* (London: Longman, Green, Long- man and Roberts, 1861).

Erbsen, Wayne. *Front Porch Songs, Jokes, and Stories: 48 Great Sing-Along Favorites.* Asheville, NC: Native Ground Music, Inc., 1993.

Erbsen, Wayne. *Log Cabin Pioneers: Stories, Songs, and Sayings.* Asheville, NC: Native Ground Music, Inc., 2001.

Hill, William E. *The Pony Express Trail: Yesterday and Today.* Caldwell, Idaho: Caxton Press, 2010.

Kincaid, Mackenzie. *The Writer's Guide to Horses; The Author's Essential Illustrated Reference to All Things Equine.* Monee, IL: Printed by Author, 2019.

McCutcheon, Marc. *The Writer's Guide to Everyday Life in the 1800s.* Cincinnati, Ohio: Writer's Digest Books, 1993.

Moody, Ralph. *Riders of the Pony Express.* Lincoln, NE: University of Nebraska Press, 1958.

Peavy, Linda and Smith, Ursula. *Pioneer Women: The Lives of Women on the Frontier.* Norman, OK: University of Oklahoma Press, 1998.

Rau, Margaret. *The Mail Must Go Through; The Story of the Pony Express.* Greensboro, North Carolina, 2005.

Swell, Barbara. *Log Cabin Cooking: Pioneer Recipes and Food Lore.* Asheville, NC: Native Ground Music, Inc., 1996.

Twain, Mark. *Roughing It.* New York: Airmont Publishing Co., 1967

Author Renée Vajko-Srch

Born to an American father and a British mother, Renée Vajko-Srch grew up in France where she obtained her French Baccalaureate. She attended IBME in Switzerland, graduating with a degree in Theology. She is a speaker with Stars for Autism, educating and training individuals and businesses about autism.

She currently lives in the Missouri Ozarks with her husband and three sons. She is a connoisseur of fine chocolates, loves to read, and has a weakness for rescue cats and Labrador Retrievers.

Renée Vajko Srch is the author of five children's books, a middle-grade historical novel, three books for adult readers, a devotional, an author workbook, and three Chicken Soup for the Soul stories. She is currently writing a mystery novel for adult readers.

She writes across the genres and for all age groups. You can follow her on her author website at www.ReneeVajkoSrch.com where you'll find her published as well as upcoming books.

You can learn more about her work at www.PenItPublications.com. She is also on Facebook (Author Renée Vajko Srch), Twitter (Renee Srch@SrchRenee), Pinterest (Author Renee Vajko Srch), and Instagram (ReneeVajkoSrch).

Illustrator Faythe Payol

Born to American missionaries in Zaire, Faythe's family fled from the rebels to France where she was raised. She obtained her Baccalaureate at the American School of Paris, attended Philadelphia College of the Bible for two years, then transferred to Huntington College in Indiana graduating with a Bachelor's degree, majoring in Art.

As a professional awarded-artist, Faythe has spent many years painting and selling her Art work in the heart of Paris where she is a member of the *Peintres du Marais*.

She teaches English, Visual Arts, and coordinates art shows for the students at the American School of Paris.

Loving mother and caring grandmother, Faythe and her husband Francis currently live in France where they enjoy spending time discovering the wonders of the countryside in Britany.

You can visit her Art gallery at www.faythe.fr

Made in the USA
Middletown, DE
29 March 2022